ESCAPE . . . OR DEATH BY DROWNING

I stumbled and fell and stayed down long enough to pull off my flippers. When I got up I began bouncing off the walls. My vision was going, and so was I. My lungs were all coughed up.

From some last reserve of strength I reached the ladder and got my hands on its rungs. In a remote region of my mind, Nick Carter was commenting, *You know, of all the spots you've been in, of all the hard ones you've come up against, there's never been one closer than this.*

"Closer!" I muttered. "I'm still not out of it!" And I wasn't. . .

From The Nick Carter Killmaster Series

NICK CARTER IS IT!

NC-A

*Dedicated to The Men of the
Secret Services of the
United States of America*

A KILLMASTER SPY CHILLER

NICK CARTER

UNDER THE WALL

CHARTER
NEW YORK

A DIVISION OF CHARTER COMMUNICATIONS INC.
A GROSSET & DUNLAP COMPANY

UNDER THE WALL

Charter Books are published by Charter Communications
a division of Grosset & Dunlap
360 Park Avenue South
New York, New York 10010

Manufactured in the United States of America

CHAPTER 1

The problem familiar: assassination attempts. The motorcade, with its police outriders, would make a right turn onto the short block flanking the north end of the park. It would pass by a grouping of four- and five-story buildings, then turn left, going down the long incline past similar buildings all on the right, and leave the plaza at its south end via the tunnel.

The crowds lining the streets and in the park area were moderately heavy. Two factors made the location ideal for a hit. The park was cluttered with formalized shrubbery in the style of an English garden with its maze of paths. It's the kind kids love to play in and the kind where a killer with a high-powered rifle can find excellent concealment. Second, the buildings that walled the route offered a clear field of fire from above.

Naturally, the scene had been checked out by the Secret Service, but it was only one point of a great many through which the motorcade would pass. And as history has shown, there is no real protection from the aim of a determined rifleman.

Like the Secret Service, AXE has its own PRS—Protective Research Section. Its job is to spot possible assassins in any location where our high-ranking officials and visiting brass might be scheduled to travel. In this case, PRS's readout through VMD Actuary indicated that there were two possible assassins in the city on the day of the motorcade. One of them had been observed frequenting the park a week before the event.

The White House passed this information on to all official agencies involved, even though it was assumed that they had developed the same profiles.

It was not something we could check out with them openly, because officially, AXE does not exist. Including the President, no more than a half dozen individuals in the federal bureaucracy know who or what AXE is. In our specialized line of business, that's the way it's got to be if AXE is to perform. It has been said that we take over where the CIA leaves off, when the party gets rough.

As Nick Carter, Killmaster N3, I know how rough that is. So does the opposition. And fortunately, while congressional committees and the press have been making mincemeat out of the CIA (to howls of laughter from the comrades at KGB headquarters, Number 2 Dzerzhinsky Street), AXE, the smallest, most secret, and most deadly arm of U.S. security, continues to operate with its usual anonymity.

The present operation was a case in point. Within the area the motorcade was now entering, fewer than fifty Secret Service, FBI, and police personnel were stationed. Unknown to them, three AXE agents were on the scene as well.

One was positioned inside a water tank on the roof of a building affording a panoramic view of the entire route. The tank was usually full of water, but for this special surveillance, it wasn't. Our man had been in place for three days. He was equipped, as were the other two agents, with a new top-secret Mark 7 laser gun and a B2 scanning device for monitoring all movement below.

A second agent was concealed on the third floor of an apartment front. His job was to monitor the line of buildings facing him across the park.

The third agent was in the park, inside a Patton tank, a World War II memorial, with a clear field of fire at the buildings known at Plaza West.

The three were in constant contact with each other and with AXE headquarters at Dupont Circle in the nation's capital.

The long line of black limousines moved slowly along the short block. The dignitaries waved and smiled, and the crowd cheered.

Projected on the AXE viewing screen the scene had a staged-in-Hollywood look—unreal. But it wasn't.

"Movement in fourth-story window, end building!" whispered the voice from the tank.

"All right, hold it," I said.

The film froze in place.

"Let's see it POV the Patton."

The scene shifted, and we were looking at the facing line of buildings as the lead car completed its turn.

"Okay, lights," I said, and the scene vanished as the lights came on.

The four trainees blinked in the glare and looked solemn.

"What order would you have given?" I asked the first.

"Shoot," he said.

"You can put your reasons in writing. You." I nodded at the second.

"I'd have held fire, at least until the Vice-President's car had made the turn."

It was a training exercise of an actual event, now two years old. You never read about it. Outside of AXE, no one ever saw the body of the would-be assassin recovered from the fourth floor of the Quinn Building after I zapped him from the tank with the Mark 7 laser.

He was a hit man with a flock of names and a nasty record. He had done jobs for a Palestinian terrorist gang, a home-grown Maoist cell calling itself Red October, and Fidel's DGI. We didn't know who had contracted him for this particular bloodletting. We did know he had arrived in the city two days before the scheduled event had been publicly announced. Our knowledge had paid off.

As a training aid, the film helped to weed out the men from the boys. In view of the background, any AXE trainee whose answer to my question did not call for direct and instantaneous action would never become an N agent. The problem was clear enough. The fourth floor of the Quinn building was supposed to be empty. You had one mission—to protect your own. You acted on that alone.

The session ended short of completion. Hawk broke it up, sending word that he wanted me in his office.

As Director and Operations Chief of AXE, David Hawk is second to none. Central Casting would never see him in the role. His nondescript rumpled suit, lean hatchet face, foul-smelling cheroot, pale blue hooded eyes, and rasping sandpaper voice did not in any way fit the standard picture of the well-pressed intelligence director. That, of course, is as it should be if intelligence is to mean anything.

Hawk was not just another face in the crowd, because he wasn't a part of it. Like AXE, he was an unknown quantity outside the cover of the Amalgamated Press and Wire Services. Behind the cover I knew him to be a tireless boss whose knowledge, perception, and sagacity combined to make AXE the espionage and intelligence arm that it is.

"Took your time getting here." He gave me his sardonic squint, knowing that although I can understand the mutual benefit of acting as a training officer between missions, operations are my meat. The diet had been lean for too long. When word to report had come, I hadn't exactly dawdled.

"I came as soon as I could, sir," I answered straight-faced.

"Sit down, Nick. We have a problem in Berlin." He blew out a cloud of rank pollution and put his hands over his belly.

I lit up one of my special gold tips in defense and waited.

"This came in from N12, Sparks, on the red channel, midnight Berlin time." He plucked the cable from his desk as he spoke.

I took it and read the decode: *Extending stay, looking into old/new mokryye dela business. Contact Kraemer on 4.62.*

"Kraemer doesn't respond, and there's no raising Sparks on any channel."

Klaus Kraemer was the long-time AXE resident in Berlin, not in the special N section but in R, which covers communications. John Sparks's message meant that Kraemer would be standing by for a followup. He wasn't.

I know the assigned locations of all N agents, and I knew N12's home base was Warsaw.

Hawk read my mind. "On Monday Kraemer requested assistance. I sent Sparks. He was due for some R and R."

"What was Kraemer's problem?"

"He didn't spell it out as a problem. Just wanted someone to stop in. It was clocked as routine."

And it was routine. Our R people are almost as few as our N. They get lonely, and it's not unusual for a request to come in for an operations type to stop by and smooth out the humps. Since N12 was due for recall, Hawk had complied.

Aside from the silence on the Berlin end, Sparks cryptic *old/new mokryye dela business* took it out of the routine. In Russian, *mokryye dela* means *blood-wet affair*, or assassination. "I'm getting rather drowned in it," I said.

"Drowned in what?" Hawk growled.

"We were just going over the San Diego film. I suppose

old/new means he's run onto an old case that may be repeated."

Hawk glared at me and nodded, smashing out the stub of his cigar before it burned his lips. "You could be right. The President called an hour ago to inform me that on his upcoming European swing, he's planning a surprise stop in West Berlin. N12 couldn't have known that, and since we aren't able to raise him we can only assume what he meant. You go get the answers, and if you find N12 alive, tell him to get his ass to this office immediately. The President will be arriving in Berlin the morning of the fifteenth."

CHAPTER 2

The quickest route to Berlin, of course, is to fly there via Frankfurt. It also makes it easy for the opposition. They put a couple of their people at Frankfurt and Templehof airports as a matter of routine. The MFS, East Germany's KGB-directed security arm, knows my face even if it doesn't know for whom I work. They'd have me spotted before I reached West Berlin's stadiumlike terminal. It would mean valuable time wasted while I shook them off. More than that, they would know I was on the scene and make my job that much tougher.

So we sacrificed some time on the front end to try to buy some security on the other. At least, that was the idea. I flew from Dulles to London's Heathrow. There I caught a British Airways Common Market shuttle to Brussels' Zaventem. I knew I was clean when I boarded a Sabena local for Hannover.

The cleanliness ended on the E8 between Hannover and the border crossing at Helmstedt. It's only a hundred kilometers—sixty miles—between the two points. But by the time I'd picked up the Belgian-registered BMW 560; in a selected slot at the Banhof, got clear of the Hannoverian traffic, and had begun cruising the autobahn, jet lag began to set in.

Jet lag is a medically recognized condition. No one can avoid it. It hits some harder than others. I'm not one of them, but AXE fatigue tests have shown that the effect dulls the fine edge of perception and reaction time—in my case, by several milliseconds. As N3 Killmaster, that could make the difference between being quick or being dead.

I carry three pieces of armament at all times. Wilhelmina, my 9mm Luger, is couched under my left arm. Hugo, my silent stiletto, is strapped to my right arm with an automatic release. And Pierre—Pierre is the *pièce de résistance,* a walnut-sized plastic egg. At rest, it resides in my shorts with a couple of other necessary friends. Pierre is usually loaded with an odorless killing gas.

None of this protection was any good to me on a long, descending, straight stretch of highway that ended in a sweeping curve above a steeply banked ravine whose pine tops came level with the road.

Again, although time was a key factor in my mission, I was willing to sacrifice a bit of it to remain unobtrusive; also, I didn't plan to make contact until the following morning. So instead of cruising the outside speed lane at 170ks, I ambled along in the center lane at an even 70 mph.

Jet lag. The mind turned inward on N12, John Sparks, a top pro in any league. The Mercedes B450SE was a mote in the eye of the rear-view mirror. It crested the rise and came down the speed lane full bore. At the moment, we were the only traffic on the stretch.

My eye said, *he's doing at least 200ks.* Judgment said the curve was too steep. He couldn't make it unless he started easing off. Or unless—!

Jet lag, and I had milliseconds to act. As I saw him start to cut toward me, my leg was a piston, hitting the brake. I had one hope. Seat belt and shoulder harness nearly popped their gussets, digging into chest and gut. Arms outthrust against the massive deceleration, neck and head fighting to stay off the wheel, I controlled the skid amid the sound of protesting rubber.

His idea had been to cut across the BMW's rear, making contact with the left side of the bumper—a kind of dainty billiard shot. As the tapped ball, I would make quite an impressive sight doing cartwheels down the autobahn, disappearing into the pine ravine at the curve. Really quite neat and simple if you know how to do it.

The billiard player missed me by about six inches—not in the rear, but in the front. I saw he needed a haircut as he struggled with his own problem, and I slapped his licence number across my memory.

In his plan to clip me he had expected to slow his own momentum. Then with the judicious use of brake and clutch, he could keep from killing himself, navigating the turn, preventing the Mercedes from going into orbit. By good luck and with superior driving he managed it, just. But not before he'd done a helluva paint- and metal-removing job along the length of the 450SE. His contact along the guard rail made a hideous screech before he fought clear and disappeared from view.

I had been picked up in Hannover. The BMW had been compromised. The pursuit had probably been signaled from the point where I had entered the E8, the tracking begun at the *parkplatz* about ten kilos back. The attempt had been professional, the result disturbing. My cover had been blown before I started.

Both Hawk and I recognized that if the problem in Berlin was connected with the President's visit, the source of the trouble was in Washington. Whatever the connection, the tipoff had come from there.

AXE needed to know that something had come loose in Hannover, and I needed a change of cars. My attacker would report his failure. His control would know I'd move to re-cover my identity. Even so, I could be sure of one thing: No attempt would be made to pick me up on the hundred-mile crossing between Helmstedt and Berlin. If that had been intended there would have been no point in trying to kill me. The reason was clear enough. Bathed in the aura of *détente,* neither the KGB nor the MFS would want to risk a nasty political incident on East German territory. They'd wait and try again when I reached West Berlin.

As a border town, Helmstedt doesn't offer much to the troops stationed there. However, up on a ridge on the north side of the town on Am Botschenberg, there's a building that looks like a school. It's a *Jungendgastehaus,* a youth hostel in the modern style. Its manager is Gunther Voss.

Voss had long been the AXE contact man on the German border. He had never heard of AXE. When he had retired from the Gehlen organization——the West German BND——in the early sixties, AXE had picked him up through a cutout system. His cover as youth-hostel manager was good. He kept his eyes and ears open and passed on border information via dead drops. And he stood ready to be of help should a salesman stop by selling hostel supplies with the comment, *I had a flat tire.*

I had made the stop once before when conditions along the border had been more active. Voss gave no hint of recognition as he came out the rear of the building into the empty courtyard, which was shielded by pine and scrub growth on both sides and backed by a long shed for cars at the rear.

I let the engine idle, watching his approach, a short, solid, grey-haired man in khaki.

"*Guten tag,*" I said.

"*Tag,*" he intoned.

"*Ich haben ein riefen defekt.*"

Voss nodded toward the empty bay at the end of the

shed. I drove the BMW into it. He was beside the door when I stepped out.

"I need a change of cars," I said.

"*Jah,* I have a Volvo DL244 you can take," he said, grabbing my travelpak as I brought out my attaché case.

"How's business?"

"Quiet."

"It could change. Get rid of the BMW."

We opened the door on the bay that housed the DL244. "Will you return it?"

"I don't know. Papers in order, green card?"

"*Jah.* Have a look.'

The Volvo was a neutral gray, the sheen worn off its newness. Voss handed me the keys. We put my equipment in the back.

I climbed in and looked up at him. "Send a priority one to KTZ," I said. "Hannover out. Check home base."

"*Jah.*"

Gunther Voss wasn't long on words. He got the message. He acted. The switch had taken no more than five minutes. In ten, I was easing along Helmstedt's Triberstrasse on the off chance that in one of the numerous garages that cluttered the street, I'd spot a Mercedes with a badly wrinkled side.

Since the attempted hit on me had happened just past the Pienne exit, the next and last place Long Hair could have pulled off was Helmstedt—that or expect to clear the West-East border check with an obviously damaged car. I didn't think he'd try that. It remained to be seen if he was smart enough to get his wreck under proper cover.

He wasn't. That or the Mercedes's rear end was shark's bait, sticking out of the garage of a body-repair shop on a narrow dead-end side street off Triberstrasse. Carelessness never pays when you're in a killing business.

I circled and parked and surveyed the afternoon scene. It appeared quiet, normal, dull. I had a good view of the side street, which wasn't much more than an alley. It ended against a cinder-block wall, backing on to a four-story building. That meant if you went in, you went out the same way—or not at all.

The repair shop and its yard took up most of one side of the street. The yard was well stocked with a jumble of banged-up vehicles, none with the stature and breeding of the Mercedes, which made it look out of place.

As I'd noted, it meant one of two things. Either Long Hair was careless, or the shop people knew him and the car's tail was sticking out in plain view on the off chance that I'd come hunting, and they could take another crack at me.

In either case, I was going hunting. Across the street from the shop on the corner of Triberstrasse there was a *gasthof,* advertising Dortmunder. I thought it a good place to start, for the inner man needed feeding and quenching.

The interior was cool and dusky with booths along the right side and a long bar along the left. At the far end was a side door that exited onto the side street. Two men sat at the bar talking to the beefy proprietor. One of the booths was occupied by a couple; the rest were empty. It was in between eating and drinking time. The three at the bar watched my approach.

"*Guten tag,*" I said. "*Toilette?*" I pointed to the rear. "*Jah, jah.*"

There was a window in the exit to the side street. As I went past I got a solid view of the body shop. Two workers were outside, one welding, the other hammering a fender. There was an office shed attached to the garage housing the 450SE. A light was on in the office, but the windows were too dirty to see detail. The john had no windows.

I returned to the bar. The two customers had departed. So had the couple in the booth. The expression on my host's face said, *Pay dirt!*

"Dortmunder, *bitte,*" I said. "Do you have anything to eat?"

He grunted, his meaty hands at work pouring the beer. "Knockwurst and potato salad."

"Good." The mirror behind the bar supplied back protection. I sat at the midpoint of the bar, giving myself time to manuever should someone unfriendly come through either door.

"You own this place?" I asked.

The bartender stood in front of me, a bulk of flesh going to fat but still powerful. Cropped salt-and-pepper hair, pads of fat under gimlet eyes, stolid expression, jowls, and belly. It all added up to SS plus thirty. "So?"

"You could use some paper towels back there."

"Sure." He shrugged, not moving from in front of me, waiting.

"How about my order?"

"Oh, sure." He began to fiddle around below the bar, but he didn't move.

I took a sip of the Dortmunder. Then the curtain went up. The side door flew open and in came the welder, hood down, gas cylinder on his back, acetylene torch in hand. The beef trust in front of me reached to grab my drinking wrist with one hand and pin my left arm to the bar. He'd do the holding while the welder did the body work.

He got the beer in his face instead, and I had him halfway over the bar when the blue-white flame of the torch snaked out.

They weren't very professional, just nasty. The idea was they'd immobilize me—maybe blind me—then pass me on to whoever had paid them off.

The bartender let out a gibbering howl as I launched him as a shield, and the torch dried the beer from his face, giving him a facial scar he'd never be proud of.

I let go of him, spun around, and went in low, driving the welder back against a booth table. I caught his torch wrist. A tongue of blinding flame arced over my shoulder. My knee in his crotch brought a muffled yell as he buckled. I tore the torch free of his hold and looked for trouble behind me.

My host, his face choleric with rage and pain, had hoisted a barstool, anxious to square matters by splattering his decor with my brains. I triggered the torch and stepped aside.

He screamed shrilly, dropping the stool and beating at his chest, trying to put out his flaming shirt. I could smell the stink of charred flesh as he staggered around, clawing at himself.

The welder, still on the floor, managed to turn off the valve on the cylinder, cutting the supply to the torch. With his other hand he produced a snub-nosed Mauser.

Before he could hurt himself with it, I kicked it out of his hand. Then I put an end to the festivities, bringing out Wilhelmina. The entire ballet had lasted about fifteen seconds. The bartender had slid down into a crouched position, hunched over himself, moaning and weeping. He was out of it.

"Get up!" I ordered the welder.

He obeyed, his breathing heavy inside the hood.

"Take it off. Not the cylinder, the mask!"

He was a big, mean-looking bastard, his pupils dilated with fear.

"Now the cylinder and the hose. Put them on the table. All right, get him on his feet, and we'll all go take a pee."

His eyes darted, looking for a way out.

"*Raus!*" I snapped.

I put the proprietor on the john in the room for *Dammen,* pants down, and locked him in. He was in shock and had nothing to offer.

The welder I placed in the room for *Herren.* "Don't give me any crap," I said, "or I'll hemstitch you so you'll look like broiled bratwurst. Who set this up?"

He blinked and swallowed. "I don't know who he is— wait!" He threw up his hands to cover his face. "I mean I don't know his name. He just shows up every now and then."

"In his Mercedes."

"*Jah! Jah!* Or some other car."

"And you and your fat pal next door do all kinds of body work for him."

"He—he pays good."

"I'll bet he does. What did he pay for this time, to kill me or just singe me a little?"

"Not to kill! Not to kill! I swear I would not kill!"

"Not unless you could get away with it. How did he know I was here?"

"He—he thought you might come. Max was told to watch and to signal if a stranger with a gray suit arrived."

"Where is he—in the office?"

He tried another swallow and jerked his head affirmatively.

"How many others over there?"

"Just Klaus. The boss went to Bielfeld."

"Turn around," I said.

His eyes flared. "No—*please!*"

I didn't have time to argue. I spun him toward the urinal and coldcocked him with Wilhelmina. He'd wake up with a sore head, surprised to be alive. He hadn't expected as much, because had the roles been reversed, he'd have finished me.

I left him on the potty too—a couple of deadbeats, lucky not to be dead.

When I went across the alley toward the office, I saw Klaus still pounding away. He was not part of the action.

With the garage-office windows as dirty as they were, I figured anyone watching the side door of the *gasthof,* seeing me step out wearing a welder's mask and equipment, would take me for the same man who had entered.

I went across the street swiftly in a half crouch, coming into the garage beside the battered Mercedes. The office entrance was near the car.

The door was open—and there was Long Hair. He turned from the window in the cluttered room with a satisfied smirk on his face. "All taken care of?"

"Not quite." My voice was muffled inside the mask as I activated the torch, stepping up into the room. He let out a whinny, going for his shoulder holster. The flame needled his hand. He tore it away with a scream, his body pivoting in a crouch.

I'd had enough of flame throwers. When he raised his head he was looking at Wilhelmina. "I won't waste time lecturing on playing with fire. Who do you work for?"

"Go to hell!" he yipped, tears of pain running down his cheeks as he gripped the wrist of his scorched hand.

I added to his misery by slashing the butt of the Luger across his face and hauling him over the desk by his laced shirt front.

"Who do you work for?" I repeated.

Spitting blood and a couple of teeth, he tried to shin kick me with the metal rim of his shoe. It made a dull clang against an oil drum. Long Hair was mean, skinny, and full of fight. He knew karate, too, and tried to use the advantage of being in close to separate me from Wilhelmina. I nearly had to separate him from his head before I got him quieted down, his face shoved against the wall, his right arm twisted up behind his back to the breaking point.

"Now we'll try again," I said. "I can break the right one first, then the left, and then your neck. Suit yourself."

"I take orders like you!" he choked. "I don't know who gives them."

"Try again."

He scrabbled and squealed, "Wait! *Wait!*"

"I don't have time."

"I'm freelance! I swear it! Calls come to my Hannover number from Romeo! I don't know who he is."

"How do you reach him?" I applied an extra centimeter of leverage. "How does he know you've made your hit?"

He was eager to explain. He called a number in Holland. Success was three rings and a hang up. Failure was five rings. He had not made the call yet. He gave me the number.

I'd come hunting Long Hair on the long shot that if I found him he'd have helpful information. But what he spat out under pain and pressure was standard form. His speciality was execution—a five-mark hit man. He'd be told who to get rid of and where, nothing else. He, like his pals across the alley, operated only for money—no ideological spirit.

I did not gently lay the butt of Wilhelmina across his heavily carpeted dome. Obviously he had not reported his failure to Romeo. If he had, he wouldn't have made a second attempt. I saved him the trouble of the call, letting the number ring three times and then hanging up.

When I looked out of the garage, Klaus, the hammer man, was nowhere in sight. Long Hair had the keys to the Mercedes in his pocket. I put him in the trunk and kept the keys. Maybe his buddy with the acetylene torch would cut him out at some point, but it would be a while before either of them was very active.

CHAPTER 3

I crossed the one-hundred-mile route between the East German border and West Berlin in light traffic at the tag end of the day. In this mellow season of *détente* all one has to do to understand what lies beneath the euphoric word is to pass over the frontier of East Germany's Stadt Wall West. It's an 840-mile-long death barrier that slashes its way north and south across the face of Europe. Guard towers, mine fields, shrapnel slings, electrified fences—you name it. And thirty-thousand Vopos to man it and make sure everything kills as it should. Its purpose is to relax tensions so that seventeen-thousand East Germans won't get wanderlust and go West.

How the Vopos behave at the checkpoint—whether it's heel clicking and smiles, or delay, search, and snottiness—depends on how well things are going up top. Usually on a day-to-day basis.

This day must have been okay, because in fifteen minutes I was cleared through, and no undue notice was taken.

The drive across gave me time for skull practice.

For obvious reasons, AXE N agents seldom work on the same mission and never associate when off a mission. Aside from the fact that our numbers are so few, like any professional espionage service AXE follows the policy of need to know. Because we take on the dirty work where the other agencies leave off, the need to know is not only to protect the agent but also to keep AXE hidden from our enemies without and our zealots within.

As N3 Killmaster, my need to know, though not as broad as Hawk's, is broader than that of any other N agent. As a result, I had backstopped N12 on two previous missions, had memorized his R file, and was totally familiar with his deep-hush mission in Warsaw.

He had been on station there for three years and was coming out because of changes of strategy. As Hawk had put it, "N12 came out clean and easy, under no suspicion. Whatever this is about, it begins in Berlin. I want it finished there before the President's visit becomes official."

With all that's been written about Berlin and its isolated Allied sector, no one on either side has seen fit to make note of the geographic difference between the two zones. West Berlin is triple the size of East Berlin. You could fit Frankfurt, Hamburg, and Munich into West Berlin and have plenty of park and woodland to spare for a population that is double that of the Eastern satrapy. The point was important to me as I passed through the vast turnpike-like Vopo clearance control into the Western zone.

During the crossing I had no way of checking out whether I was under surveillance. Now, surging up from Glienicker Bruke, I swung off Konigstrasse, deciding to find out. For the next half hour I cruised the woodland roads around the Wannsee, moving through the Grunewald with an eye on my rear-view mirror, the side roads, even keeping a check above me for helicopters.

By the time I'd circled past the Olympia Stadium in Charlottenburg and eased down some back streets on to

Kurfürstendamm, I was certain that whatever orders Long Hair had failed to carry out, his employers were not yet aware that I was in West Berlin.

Moving through the early-evening traffic toward the stub of the Kaiser Wilhelm Kirche was the like snapping the final item on a checklist into place. It said that bright, gay West Berlin was not only a historical and political monument to idiocy, but also the most dangerous hunting ground on the flaccid face of western Europe. You could start with the location and go on from there, but there wasn't any need. Just view the colorful tinsel of Kurfürstendamm and then the bomb-blasted Kirche, and if you didn't figure the score, you never would and it wouldn't matter anyway.

It mattered to me and to my boss back on Dupont Circle for purely practical reasons.

The hotel was on a tree-shaded *platz* not far from the Zoo Station and the Tiergarten. Within the sprawl of the Free University campus, it had a slightly run-down look glossed over with a phony air of top service, catering to special clientele. Like any hotel in West Berlin, it was a front for whatever the traffic would bear, or it was exactly what the innocent visitor assumed it to be.

In my case I knew that Fritz, one of the porters, was a BND informant, reliable for a price, and that the garage attendant, Zitor, was reliable, period. AXE had selected this hotel for these reasons plus the fact that staying at the Osdorf fitted my cover as newsman. The Youth Forum I had come to cover was an old event, trotted out on a more or less annual basis for the usual propaganda mileage.

Until this latest fandango, every time the Communists had hoisted the slogans high in a Western capital, the results had not been very joyous for them, so the routine had been to unfurl the banners in Eastern capitals, where the results could be kept under control. Now for the first time the gala week of sporting events, parades, and prop-aganda was to be hosted by the students and faculty of the Free University of West Berlin, who were eagerly preparing to welcome the Eastern faithful.

Zitor had not been expecting me. He didn't know me from Adam. He just knew, when I mentioned he might check my oil and use a Benzo Kol if I needed any, that I was a friend whom he was to help should the occasion arise. Zitor had begun his career in Budapest at fifteen, helping to litter the area around Gellert with Russian tanks. He'd been helping ever since.

When I stepped out of the lift into the concave hotel foyer I took in the usual jumble of the newly arrived clustered around the check-in desk. The concierge and two assistants were hard at it, sorting them out. The lobby's décor was heavily overdone with the Youth Forum's worn motif of Friendship, Brotherhood, and Anti-imperialism. I saw it as an interruption to be avoided. I left the formalities of registration to Fritz, who knew me no better than Zitor but recognized at once the distinctive GRD lapel button I was sporting. It stood out for him like a stop sign at the Grand Prix.

"Room 324," he sighed through his thatched moustache, his breath a rancid bouquet of pilsner and horseradish. The glint in his eye was counting marks.

I handed him my bag, moving toward the circular stairway to avoid the elevator, figuring I was going to slide through the flotsam without becoming a part of it.

"Nicholas *liebchen!* Oh, Nikky!"

I got halfway around before she had her hands on my shoulders, her lips streaking my jaw.

My inner reactions were obvious: fury at being so easily compromised, concerned that it had been so easy.

As I faced her, the tumblers in my mind were clicking at full speed. It's always necessary in my business to assume the improbable and to make contingency plans to meet it. Often, how well the plans are laid determines whether you stay alive.

In Long Hair's case, anything I had assumed about his actions after he had failed to kill me became meaningless once I reached West Berlin. I drove a different car than he could have reported. I had changed my appearance enough between Helmstedt and Glienicker Bruke—blond wig, steel-rimmed glasses with forged passport to match—and reverted again in Osdorf's garage so that I would bet my life, as I have often enough, that I had not been tailed to the hotel.

Yet here, with her fine, strong arms around my neck, her fine flank against my thigh, her lovely lips seeking mine, was proof that I was wrong. Or was it just a happy coincidence that out of the two million plus citizens of the Western zone of Berlin, on an evening in July, Nick Carter and Lola Steinmetz had met by chance in a hotel that under any circumstance approaching normal they would have avoided? Me, because as an AXE agent my usual residence in Berlin was the safe house at 10 Holgenstrasse. And Lola, as a BND officer, would never have been injected into such an obvious circus of East-West agitprop. No intelligence agency—particularly the BND—would be so stupid. Yet by God, here she was, three years since our last encounter! A golden brown Rhine maiden, wanting guests and hotel personnel to know she had found her Siegfried, Nick Carter. My immediate reaction was that by calling me by name she had set me up. For now or later?

To guard against now, I played to her act, caught her off her feet, swung her around, my lips brushing her cheek.

I glimpsed amused expressions, plus the hard eye of Fritz, and by the time I set her down, I had my back against the stairway pillar and a fairly good view of the infield.

"Oh, Nicholas, I never would have dreamed it! Is it really you?" She played it perfectly, a bit breathless, enchanted, her magnificent frontage rising on its own tide.

I had always remembered how clear her blue eyes were against the gold of her hair. She had the high cheekbones of the northern raider. Nothing had changed, it seemed, but the sides. BND for Lola had become MFS.

"Lola, Lola, I've been driving all over Berlin looking for you." I kept my hands on her shoulders, holding her in place.

She made no effort to get away, her eyes wide with a puckish excitement. "Oh, what do you mean by that?" She was good, all right. I remembered that, too. Her signal had been to identify me, not to set me up for the hit here.

"Why, to take you to dinner, of course."

We had a big laugh and another hug over that one. And with it I was able to double-check the balcony and see that no one was paying any attention to us.

"Seriously, what are you doing in a place like this?"

"You've heard of inflation—the marks, the dollar. I have an editor who thinks this is just the place."

"Now really, Nikky, I—"

"And what, may I ask, are you doing here"—I looked her over carefully—"all dressed up? And don't tell me you're waiting for me to take you to dinner."

"Oh, I have a silly little sister, Helga, who is staying here to take part in the Youth Forum. She could stay with me, but she insists upon staying with her comrades." The color rose in her face, and she looked genuinely annoyed.

"College student?"

"What else?"

"Let her have her fun."

"Ach, they know so little. They know nothing but prattle."

"Shall we take her out and teach her a thing or two?"

Her reaction was a little too swift. "Oh, no! No, she'd never come. I came to invite her for a drink. Too busy. Her group is having a planning session."

"Well, then there's no escaping the situation."

"What do you mean?"

"We'll simply have to go and have that dinner, and you

can tell me what you've been doing with yourself ...
since an October too long ago."

"A red October," she said, and there was no smile,
forced or real, left on her lovely face, as her fingers
tightened around mine.

I didn't invite her to my room while I changed my tie. I
wanted to see her reaction. Was she in a hurry? Was this
to be a quick kill, as had already been attempted on me,
or was this to be an evening out with some spoilsport
interrupting the bed-romping conclusion?

She gave me her cagey I-agree-let's-not-rush-it-darling
smile when I said, "Look, I need a shower and a shave.
Suppose I pick you up in an hour, at your place or wherever."

"Wonderful, *liebchen*," she said, and patted my arm.
"It's so good to see you, Nikky." It came out smoothly,
teasing.

"No more than you, I hope, darling. Where and
when?"

CHAPTER 4

In the shower, I reflected. It had been a red October, beginning on the seventh with the supposed joint suicides of Major General Horst Wendland, acting Vice-President of the BND, and Admiral of the Fleet Hermann Ludke, and finishing on the thirty-first with the discovery of the Rhine-washed body of Gerhard Bohn, a senior defense official. In all there had been nine "suicides" between those dates, and all the departed had been employed by the Federal Republic in high, medium, or low positions. Unknown to the German public, but of considerable importance to Western intelligence agencies, was the fact that along with Wendland and Ludke, the other seven had been BND connected.

AXE interest in the case was only incidentally focused on who was using suicide as a method to reduce the BND's overstaffed ranks. Our concern was that Admiral Ludke, whose suicide was unique (while hunting near the Belgian border, he had managed to shoot himself twice in the back with a bolt-action rifle), had been wired in on

31

some special AXE R&D on a weather-modification weapons system. Just before his suicide we had learned that the admiral was a double agent for KGB–MFS. My job had been to find out whether the WM information had been turned over to an MFS resident in Bonn and to take appropriate action. Lola's mission had been to find out whether the admiral's aide, Captain Von Rentlow, or his Secretary, Frau Weigle, was also playing the double game.

In retrospect—or in any respect—the most satisfying part of the action had been Lola. You'd have to swim a long way before you'd find a Niebelungen to match her magic, astride or afloat. She had had no idea what my bag was. She simply knew me as an American military agent posing as a newsman. And I had known that she was Lola Steinmetz, employed as a secretary to Wendland's opposite number, but actually BND agent R-32, code name Rudi Best. We knew we were on the same side, and for cover, ours was one of those sudden romances, a cover we emphasised to the hilt.

Okay, that was an Ocktoberfest of fun and games, amid some fast back-alley butchery. This was a later day, and my playmate of yesteryear had just managed to blow my cover all over the lobby of an East-West gathering.

In my business when unexpected contact is made, you have to know whether it's better to break it or tighten it. As with Long Hair, I knew I had to tighten it because I was operating essentially in the dark with nothing much to go on, and to break away would be to add to the darkness and narrow my area of operations. Whatever Lola knew, she was going to tell me, one way or the other.

Her quick acceptance of my invitation was as much an act as her greeting. But she knew that just as soon as we parted I'd be in the position to start checking on her, so even if she failed to keep the date, I'd have a line on her actions. So her instructions were either to play along to set me up or, on the strength of our past relations, to lock me in the vise of her golden thighs and, with all the rhythm and subtlety of her kind, pump me dry of whatever she was after. It was the kind of interrogation two could enjoy.

I left the hotel on foot and walked to the Zoo Station, where I called Paul Wehner from a kiosk.

"Wehner." The bass voice had lost none of its resonance.

"Paul, Nick Carter here."

There was no hesitation. I might have spoken to him five minutes ago instead of two years. "Good of you to call."

"I just got in. I wanted to get in touch with Rudi. Do you have his number? I've lost it."

"Sure, if you want to call Pasau. He's on holiday."

"Know when he'll be back?"

"Never!" he laughed. "Anything I can do?"

"I'm here on a story on the East-West forum. I thought Rudi might have some background."

"I've got a file as thick as your head. You're welcome to go through it."

"Good. I'll call you tomorrow—maybe we can have lunch."

"My pleasure, Nick."

Paul Wehner's official job was press-information editor for the West Berlin branch of the Social Democratic Party (SPD). Unofficially, he was the Federal Republic's BND chief of station for West Berlin. More than that, he was a trusted friend. I had once saved his life.

Translated, his information had more or less reaffirmed what I had figured. Lola was no longer with BND. Nothing indicated she had switched sides. He would look into it.

This last was no surprise either. For the past ten years BND had had a pretty lousy efficiency record. Its failure had brought down Willy Brandt when it was learned through outside intelligence assistance that Brandt's closest advisor, Gunther Guillame, was a longtime East German MFS agent.

What saved BND from being totally second rate were professionals like Paul Wehner, and fortunately it had a fair share of them.

Lola's flat was in a quietly expensive section of Schmargendorf, two blocks fron the Heidelberg Platz. I came to it with care, and as I rang the chimes I was relatively sure that no one was going to try to put an end to the evening before it got started.

If nothing else fitted with Lola, her dress did. It was difficult to tell where it began and she ended. They went together in a way that made her clothes necessary only for their removal.

"You like it, *liebchen?*" She had a chuckle that rendered conversation unnecessary.

"I like it very much. Here's a yellow rose to go with your hair."

We walked slowly together the short distance to the car, and no one tried to shoot me, although I could understand the thought.

She saw the Volvo. "I've got a new Mercedes. We could take that," she said, teasing.

"Not the girl I remember in Bad Godesberg," I said sadly. "When we were together, walking was good enough."

She laughed and hugged my arm. "Oh, Nikky, you haven't changed. I still can't get over our meeting."

"We'll take our time and you'll get used to it."

In the car I offered her my cigarette case with my gold-tip specials.

She reacted to the case, her hand on it, looking at me. "I do remember." She took a cigarette. "I'm out of that business. I left it right after."

"And business is now much better?" I held the lighter for her.

"Oh, much!" she chuckled, the seriousness gone. "You wait and see what a poor working girl can do. I'll tell you all about it."

We dined at Huberts in Charlottenburg, not only because the food was worth the inflated price, the Reisling inspired, but also because it was a place she could tell me all without fear of interruption. I knew we hadn't been followed, but for the moment it didn't matter, because Huberts, a perfectly legitimate restaurant, is also a British SIS club, and he who belongs can be assured of sipping his Moselle in both privacy and safety.

The answer to Lola's newfound affluence was normal, plausible, almost routine, and smelled of old scrod.

"Nikky, believe me, I was so tired of it, so sick of the idiots and the idiocy, so when Winty—he's a dear, you'll love him—made me the offer, how could I turn it down?" She gestured, the movement accentuating the swell of her breasts so that the nipples were momentarily the focal point of every male in the place. "Besides, you disappeared without a goodbye, without anything. You could have at least sent a postcard." She pouted.

"What do you call your place—Lola's?"

"Don't be gauche, *leibchen*. Treadeau's. I'm right on the corner of Kurfürstendamm and Spichernstrasse. It's a perfect location."

"Wouldn't Munich or Frankfurt or even Cologne be a more lucrative spot for a French fashion boutique than poor old forgotten West Berlin?"

"Forgotten, nothing! Maybe politically forgotten, which is fine, because with *détente,* all those party *milch* cows from the East can come here more easily. And come they do! Who ever heard of buying Mainbocher in a people's republic? They're getting fat and rich over there, and their East marks are beginning to look almost as good as West, so"—she threw out her hands—"I'm a lover of *détente.* I trade with the enemy. I sell them pantyhose and lingerie and all kinds of pretty French things. And believe me, I make them pay."

There was no doubting Lola's enthusiasm or her German interest in a good business deal. Her shop would be sleek and smart, a perfect East-West contact point delicately perfumed and glossed over with sexy French chic.

"Sounds terribly dull and successful, my love. Tell me about—what's his name?—Winty?"

"Oh, he's fabulous! Terribly successful himself. He wants me to marry him, naturally. Magnus Torsten von Winterberg. Very old German family from Silesia."

"Which is now a part of Poland."

"Which is now a part of the past." She said it firmly, a touch of annoyance in her electric eyes.

"Everything is a part of the past, honeychild, even our meeting."

She almost ran with it, then caught herself and patted my hand. "Yes, but as a result, this is now, and that's all I'm interested in. You know, I have a wicked idea." The candlelight on her shadowed face was perfect for a wicked idea.

"I can see it," I said, thinking, *Now we come to phase two.*

"There's a discotheque I've heard about called M'Efoe's. It's said to have the naughtiest floor show in town. Winty is too much of a prude to take me. Would you like to?"

"Definitely not. It might spoil your reputation."

"Or improve my technique."

"That would be an impossibility."

"Oh, how sweet you are," she purred, running her finger down the back of my hand.

"Where do we find this devil's den?"

"It's in the Tiergarten, of all places."

"Sounds strange enough." It sounded obvious, too.

I had no intention of taking her to M'Efoe's, the victim of an erotic hit, but I did want to see the place simply for reference, and I did want to see her reaction when I drove

on by and headed for Wannsee. I planned to park by the
lake for a serious chat in which I would explain that I
considered it a bit insulting to be taken to watch some
Nubian princess being screwed by a mountain goat when
we had much better things to do.

Instead, it was our night for more of the unexpected.
Code intro be damned, I did have *ein reifen defekt*—a
flat!—right in the middle of Kaiserdamm. I slowed and
edged the wounded Volvo toward the curb. The thoroughfare was heavy with traffic, every driver behind me
furious that something had slowed his rush to nowhere.
While I did my easing, Lola laughed good-naturedly and
gestured sadly at my effort to get the Volvo off the track
before we were rammed. "Next time we'll take the
Mercedes," she said.

I managed to ease into an emergency *platz*, and then it
was the routine of police, tow truck, and cab. German efficiency does not permit changing a tire on a main *strasse*,
partly to keep you from being run over, but mostly because it's good business for service stations and taxis.

Fifteen minutes later, in a taxi, Lola asked, "Where are
we going?"

"A little club I know. Wickedest show in town." I
rested my hand on her silken knee.

"But this isn't the way to the Tiergarten." She laid her
hand over mine.

"You're right, *leibchen*. I know a better club, much
quieter, more privacy. I own it for the night."

"But. . .!" Her fingers stiffened, then lifted. "But,
Nicholas! . . . Oh, you're as bad as Winty!"

"I'll try to correct that." I was interested in gauging her
reaction.

In retrospect, she acted beautifully, her only counter-
suggestion being that we go to her place instead of mine.

We had an after-dinner—after-flat, we called it—
brandy in a small, intimate bar full of dull marble tops
and dark wood. During it, Fritz was instructed to see to

the disgraced Volvo, and Lola looked pensive and magnetically seductive.

The connection between us had been building since our first touch. As we rose, the electricity between us made her seem to glow and, if possible, her dress to cling even more closely. Lola, I decided, had accepted unexpected conditions over which she had so control and, professional that she was, was going to make the most of them in the best way she knew.

The first time, I took her so hard and fast I left her literally stunned. She lay on the bed, clothing neither on nor off, thighs spread, her magnificent breasts heaving, eyes wide and glazed, her breath coming in choked sobs. "Ohhh, Ni-kky!" she kept moaning.

I covered her mouth with mine, smothering the little cries, and began the long, steady buildup, no hurry now. Intensity was the name of the game. We reached it by slow, tantalizing degrees. Lips on nipples, tongue on thighs, fingers moving, grasping, stroking. In the soft darkness her golden head rose and fell rhythmically. I had to move away. She moaned and sighed broken words as my lips moved up the long length of her leg. I tasted her heat and she cried out, her fingers fastened in my hair. She began to ask for it, tugging at me to rise. I did so in my own good time, and by that time Lola had become the wildest Rhine maiden of them all. We played who's on top and who's astride and who's my stallion now. And when we exploded together she was bent like a bow, knees gripping my flanks, fingers fastened on my buttocks, my hands beneath hers, the arrow locked in the target.

CHAPTER 5

You don't have to see fear; you can smell it. I could both see it and smell it in the face and form of Horst Lutz, attendant at the Museum Haus am Checkpoint Charlie. He came down the stairs to the museum's central foyer, looking like Banquo's ghost with the faint yet pervasive stink of the grave about him.

Lutz was my sole AXE contact, and a very thin one at that. A former East German Vopo, he had escaped in 1972. His uncle was Klaus Kraemer. Kraemer, stationed at a key collecting post, badly needed an errand boy whom he could trust. In 1975, after an exhaustive checkout, AXE gave the green light, and his nephew, without ever knowing for whom he was working, began doing odd jobs for his uncle.

Lutz was an escapee and former border guard, and his employment at the Museum, within spitting distance of the Berlin Wall, brought him in contact with thousands of visitors from everywhere. This made him readily accessible for contact under a legitimate cover. On his own, we

knew he had been involved in a couple of escape operations, helping others cross from the East. This, too,
opened up some possible future use by AXE. But in
working for his uncle, Lutz had no real information beyond the low-level jobs he was assigned on a need-to-
know basis, and the need was very little.

So I wasn't expecting much out of him. His obvious
fear came as a pleasant surprise. It was far more of a
straight signal than Lola's eager approach.

He was escorting a small group of sightseers down the
stairs, explaining a wall display of photographs, when he
spotted me examining an escape vehicle. Although he
managed not to succumb to it completely, the shock of
recognition was obvious, and his hand abruptly gripped
the bannister. I didn't like that, even though he didn't
know me. What he did know was the pale gray suit, the
folded copy of *Die Welt* in the left pocket of my jacket,
and the hour of 1100, which was the standard time of the
particular day for an official caller to make contact.

There were few visitors taking the tour, and when I
went up the stairs and moved about I saw that the area
was largely vacant. Lutz was tall and powerfully built. His
voice was deep, and its sound did not betray his inner
feeling. That was good. But he was scared about something.

I strolled around, expecting him to show up, letting my
thoughts look over my back trail. I had taken Lola home
in the gray dawn. She had been weary and withdrawn, a
little sad, and anxious to see me again soon. Our encounter had cost me nothing. Whatever the plan had been, it
had not worked out. Her failure might bring an overreac-
tion on the part of her control. At least they knew I was
going to be a worry.

To stimulate it, I had left the hotel on the floor of
Zitor's old Mercedes, a really vintage model. He had
dropped me at the S-Bahn, and I had gone through a
series of direct reversals, including two cups of coffee and

some delicious homemade buns before I boarded a tour
bus to the museum and the Wall.

The museum was a result of the Wall. It was lodged in
a tumbledown three-story house that in better days had
been a popular café and whorehouse. Now it featured a
photographic history of the city's division, along with all
sorts of objects and records of escape from the East, some
successful, some not. It was a relic of the cold war, and
millions of tourists had passed through its door. I didn't
expect it would stay open much longer. It didn't fit in
with the image of *détente*.

Neither did Lutz, who came into the room where I was
standing with a new party of tourists. His eyes cried out
a warning. "Of course," he said to a dungareed blond
beside him, "the answer is in the escape vehicle's hood.
The fact that three people were fitted under it shows the
kind of determination of which I am speaking."

The three with him were not the danger his eyes
flashed, nor was the female attendant at the entrance desk
below. I was sure of that. I went on downstairs and
browsed there, waiting to see who would come. No one
did. The warning lay elsewhere, perhaps unseen in the
maze of little rooms and corridors of the old cathouse. An
answer of sorts could be under the hood of the escape
car. Horst might look and stink of fear, but he could keep
his head.

The vehicle was a very low-slung homemade job, low
enough to pass under the steel barrier at the checkpoint.
The engine had been shifted to the rear, and the hood
had concealed people instead of horsepower.

I stood in front of the machine. No one was paying attention to me as I raised the hood. I saw nothing but the
empty hiding space. Then I looked down and saw the
edge of crumpled paper sticking out of the disconnected
radiator hose, a key wrapped in it.

I left the building knowing I was fair game for gun or
camera focused on the building front from the East side
of the Wall as well as from the West. The allied check-

point was just to my right in the center of Friedrichstrasse. Off to the right at the Wall was an official reviewing stand. Facing me were a line of three- and four-
story buildings. They ended at Zimmerstrasse, which was
a narrow fronting street parallel to the Wall. It was really
a lousy place for an AXE agent to pay a call. Maybe it
was so lousy, it was good. No one would believe it. At
least, no one followed me back to the Osdorf.

There was a message from Lola asking me to call. But
the message I'd picked up from Lutz was far more to the
point. In his scrawl was written, "3rd floor, 18 Zimmerstrasse 2000 hrs." And under the line there was another
address. "69 Schützen." It wasn't the address that held
me, but the handwriting. I recognized N12's bold stroke.

69 Schützen was in the Eastern zone, two blocks from
the Wall off Friedrichstrasse in an extremely exposed location. But I wasn't going near it before I'd had a talk
with Lutz. In the meantime, there was Paul Wehner to
see.

We met in a quiet café near the radio tower. "You
don't change," was his dry greeting.

"Nor you." I felt the strength of his hand. Square face,
dusty blond hair, observant eyes, a droll twist to his
mouth, as though it was all so foolish, and behind the
placid look, a keen mind that knew how to reach swift
conclusions and take direct action. Or so I had remembered him.

"How's business?"

"Busy season. I'll have a Dortmunder, blond."

"Good. Make that two and in the stein," he said to the
waiter.

"Tell me about our friend. Why did she leave?"

"No overriding reason. Got tired of it. Lots do." I detected a sardonic note.

"And for good reasons these days."

"Exactly."

"And so her friend von Winter set her up in business as well as in a place with a nice view."

"And she's done well since."

"How has he done, what does he do?"

"Sells steel tubing, metal castings to the East."

"No Western customers?"

"Oh, sure, but either way it's all legitimate, as far as we have been able to tell."

"I think I'd have another look." Like so many things of late it seemed too obvious to be a setup, which for some reason made the possibility genuine.

"Anything you can tell me?"

"I just have. Lola and her boyfriend are doing more than selling *chapeaux* and castings to our newfound friends."

Wehner shrugged. "Von Winter was a tank commander in the Western Desert, captured in forty-three. Never political, strictly business."

"Yeah, I know. I'm going to give you an address. I need to know its significance, what it is, plus a detailed physical description. I need it soon as possible."

"How soon?"

"By tonight when I call you, sometime around nine."

"See what I can do. What's the address?"

I gave it to him. "Is this a safe place?"

He raised his eyes, alert.

"The one on the end, he's had his eye on us."

Wehner chuckled and relaxed. "Not very good. He's one of mine. I'll tell him, give him hell."

"Good idea." I offered him one of my cigarettes. "There's one other thing. If the police have any unidentifiables in the morgue picked up in the last forty-eight hours, I'd like to see them."

Wehner grunted, sipping his beer. "Say when."

"When."

"Anything else?"

"Yeah, how the hell are you, and let's have something to eat."

I couldn't put my finger on it, but I'd been wrong on one count. Paul Wehner had changed. Before my departure from headquarters Hawk and I had held a brief skull session on Kraemer. There were only two reasons why he would have broken contact. Either he was dead or he was in the hands of the opposition. He had not been injured in some normal manner. Had that happened, his nephew had been instructed to place an ad in the *Berlin Morgenpost*. But whether he was dead or alive, I couldn't move in his direction until I'd talked to Horst. At least, I couldn't move in the normal manner.

"I have a final request," I said to Wehner as he stubbed out his cigarette. "I want to go flying."

"The question is where," he sighed.

"Oh, just routine. A slingwing ride—only on the West side, of course."

"Routine police patrol?"

"Better if it was one of those advertising jockies. Buy Joe's Weinerschnitzel, something like that."

"When?"

"After we finish our coffee." He didn't return my smile.

CHAPTER 6

The pilot's name was Freddie. Big, bushy haired, grinning type. I was introduced as an American news photographer, wanting to get some contrast shots between the zones. I was using a Hasselblad 500 with a five-inch lens, so I assured him there was no need to get too close to the Wall as he flew his Goeben Shoes route.

Because of the heavy aerial traffic the chopper's flight pattern was stiffly prescribed. Three-hundred meters altitude on a three-kilo-by-five-kilo course. The craft was a noisy, antiquated tandem type of German vintage. The racket kept our conversation to a shouted minimum, which was fine. Freddie liked to sing, either to overcome the sound or to add his off-key baritone to the noise. I thought it was going to work out fine until we had flown the pattern twice, and I had clicked off some inocuous views of activity below. Then I realized that not from any angle on the course could I spot 16 Lippanslaan Lane.

Kraemer was a watchmaker by trade. His shop faced on to an old prewar lane lined with other craft shops.

Completely leveled during the war, it had been rebuilt in its former style. In the rebuilding, AXE had seen to it that there was a false backing on Kraemer's place, which was the end shop and the largest on the lane. Within the concealed area Kraemer had his transmitting and receiving equipment. It was constantly being updated, to the point that even the Soviet Embassy in Washington could offer nothing more sophisticated.

Berlin was a major AXE listening post. If we lost the post, it would not be the end of the world, nor would its discovery expose its ownership, any more than Kraemer's exposure would reveal his actual employer. But because of what had happened, I felt it imperative to have a look at the place without attracting attention. Under the present flight conditions there was no way. I scribbled Freddie a note—"Could you change easterly heading to 95 degrees on next goround?" He grinned hugely, shook his mop, and tried shouting his reply, gesturing with his hands, the slingwing bouncing merrily along.

"Very important," I wrote on the paper. "Only need one pass."

Freddie was the stubborn type. He continued to shake his head, wave, and sing, pointing straight ahead.

I am patient when necessary. It was no longer. Besides, Freddie knew the request for me to ride along amid the neon of Goeben Shoes had come from above. He wanted to show who was boss.

"Just once," I scrawled at the bottom of the page. "I'll buy you a beer."

Again the clownish hard-to-get act. I put a stop to it as he brought the chopper onto its easterly track, touching his shoulder with Wilhelmina and then pointing the Luger at the gyro compass.

He did the usual freeze, double-take routine, the smile fading from his face.

"One pass!" I shouted. "Ninety-five degrees!"

He started to protest.

"*Now,* goddammit!"

He jerked away as I dug Wilhelmina into his back. He brought the chopper on to the proper heading, his head beginning to swivel as though expecting an immediate attack from a squadron of F-104s.

"Relax, Freddie. This won't take a minute."

"You can't fly this thing!" He was starting to get his nerve back. "You shoot me with that and—!"

"And it'll hurt like hell, if I don't kill you. And yes, I can fly this bird, so don't give me the opportunity."

"But this is forbidden! It's dangerous! We're outside the prescribed course! We can't—!"

"Shut up and fly!"

We were coming up on the district. The angle was about right. There were a gaggle of tall buildings and then beyond them, tucked in, Lippanslaan.

"Go down to two hundred meters." I punctuated the request with Wilhelmina's snout.

He grunted angrily and eased the yoke forward.

I was sitting on an angle behind him. I put the Luger in my belt and lifted the binoculars. For a second I couldn't get the orientation placed. Something was out of whack. Then I got it. We went right on past the target, but not before I'd had time to drop the binoculars and raise the camera for some fast shots. What they would show would be the lane with its three end buildings gone. They'd been burned to the ground.

About that time I got a chance to prove to Freddie that I knew how to handle his flying shoe tree. The *spat* of the plexiglass bubble taking a puncture was a dulled sound over the engine's racket and Freddie's shocked cry. His hands went to his head. As he slumped over I saw the bright red between his clenched fingers and felt the chopper shake under the effects of ground fire. There was no chance to spot where the firing was coming from. The main rotor had been hit. It was out of sync, and we were falling off, starting to plunge to the left, the vibration building toward self-destruction.

I came across Freddie, slantwise, hands reaching for

the collective and the cyclic. There was no way to get to the rudders to control the yaw. There wasn't time anyway. I'd spotted a schoolyard with its protective buildings, and I was coming down into it in a wild skid. I decreased the rpm for the moment and eased the collective down, hoping to cut some of the vibration. The ground was swinging up in a helluva fashion. It was flare time, now or never. I eased back on the cyclic stick, went clockwise on the rpm, and kept lowering the collective. It wasn't really complicated—it was just that the damn thing was practically out of control and I was trying to fly it over Freddie's back.

The best thing about the landing was that we missed the trampoline and no one was in the schoolyard. At the last second I cut all power, and we dropped in hard, skidding across the cement. The blades of the still unwinding rotor made contact with a metal light pole, which filled the air with flying metal and a helluva clatter. The contact also prevented us from wiping out the landing gear and going over on our side, which could have meant all kind of nasty business with fire and smoke and even louder noises.

Instead, I was out of the battered bird while it was still squawking and chattering and had Freddie on my back, clear of the thing before it gave its last gasp.

Freddie was more blood and shock than anything serious. He'd taken a graze, and he would have a vicious headache, which would be made worse by trying to explain what had happened.

As police and crowd began to gather on the run, I established that I was just an innocent stroller who had happened by as the chopper had fallen out of the sky. As the excitement and confusion mounted, I slipped away.

CHAPTER 7

One thing was certain—whoever had shot us down had known I was on board. They had known it in time to set up a rifleman in the burned-out wreckage of Klaus Kraemer's former post, knowing that was where I wanted to go. That meant that Nick Carter had been under close surveillance even though I was sure I had been clean from the time I departed the Osdorf to make contact with Horst Lutz.

It was Wehner who had set up the helicopter ride. But he'd made the arrangement by phone and had not accompanied me to the pad. I had gone by taxi to the general area and the rest of the way on foot.

There are two kinds of surveillance—one visual, the other electronic. At the moment, I could rule out neither. It was damned disturbing. As N3, I hadn't survived by being unable to determine one of the basic criteria of espionage. I knew I'd better determine it damned fast.

I headed for the nearest *Stadtbad*—public bath. There, I rented a private cubicle and stripped down. I made a

thorough investigation of all my clothing and every item
in it. Then I examined self. Clothing was clean. Self was
not.

On the lower side of my left buttock was attached a
wafer-thin, dime-shaped sticking plaster. Some sticking
plaster—a fly-weight homing device with a transmitting
capacity to pick up voice communication. Neat. Since
Lola had got her lovely hands on me, I'd been a walking
encyclopedia. It wasn't the time or place, but I couldn't
help but laugh like hell—a highly sophisticated electronic
melody played on a very old theme. Talk about being
tailed!

I decided to chalk up my carelessness to jet lag. I hated
to think what Hawk would chalk it up to.

I sat in the cubicle retracing all my moves since Lola
and I had broken contact. They would know I had been
to the museum at Checkpoint Charlie. No words had been
exchanged there. The bug, actually a minutely miniatur-
ized 27V transistor, could hear, but it couldn't see. So
while location and conversation had been monitored,
physical identity had not. I had not been seen meeting
Wehner. I had not been seen going to the launch pad, and
that was the best I could say for my travels, which was
damn little. They'd had me boxed in the sling wing, and
they knew exactly what I had in mind. What they had in
mind was a hit, and again they'd just missed.

In my business there is no room for error and less for
recriminations. If you survive the error, you have two
choices: to see that it doesn't happen again or to turn it
to your own advantage. I didn't have time to confuse the
opposition by heading off on a tangent, like going out to
Templehof and flying to Munich where I could leave the
beauty mark with a friend at Radio Free Europe who
could broadcast the lastest news on *détente* into it with a
little Beethoven thrown in. A transmitter as sensitive as
Lola's required equally sensitive receiving equipment.
Either the receiver was fixed in someone's ear or it was
hooked up on a control network where it was being moni-

tored by an operator. In either case, extreme sensitivity was the word, and I suited my actions to it carefully.

Whoever was doing the monitoring would have tracked me from the downed chopper to the *Stadtbad*. The thinking would be that I was banged up, wanted to avoid questioning, and needed to repair the damage. There was one conclusion to that. They'd be sending someone to finish the job—and right now. Each cubicle had its own locker. I put everything but Wilhelmina in mine. I draped my towel over the Luger with delicacy, because she now had a bugged barrel. Then I left the cubicle for the steam. At that hour of the day its only occupants were a couple of oversized beer guzzlers, lying on benches, looking like overripe seals in the heat.

I didn't have long to wait. I was pleased to see they thought well enough of me to send two to do a man's work. Big, square-headed, no-neck types. One ambled over to the steam valve and increased the flow. The other sat down in the corner across from me. Neither carried towels. This was to be a hands and feet job. The steam thickened.

When it was thick enough, the one across from me would make his move. The pool was on my right. I couldn't see either of them as I slipped off the bench and into the frigid water without a ripple, adjusting to the sudden change. I began edging along the pool's rim, and halfway down it, I spotted the foot and leg of number one. He was moving toward where I was supposed to be.

There was no time for introductions. I thrust out both hands, grasped his ankles, and with my feet braced on the side of the pool, launched him into it with a muscle-bending jerk. He came in like a baked halibut, with hardly a chance to yell before his head was under.

The pool wasn't deep, no more than six feet at the far end. By the time I had him under I was behind him, my fingers locked on the pressure points of his jugular, my legs clamped around his. He strained desperately, his fingers tearing at mine, his legs fighting to break free. I gave him no chance. Nothing. Just all the killing pressure I could exert.

In thirty seconds, he had stopped struggling. In thirty-five I knew his lungs were full of water, his body gone limp. In forty I was out of the pool, looking for his partner. He was standing by the side of the pool, worried, wondering what had happened. I could just make out his pinkish hide.

"Herman?" he grunted as I stood up.

"*Jah*. The water is good."

"Humm." It was a grunt. "You went in fast."

"I had company."

"Ahhh!"

"Please shut up, muttered one of the steamers. "I'm trying to sleep."

"Well then, go home to bed."

I reached the bench and pulled my towel out from under it. He came up behind me in the steam, and as I swung around, I saw the doubting look on his face. He saw my face, cursed, and moved fast. Not fast enough.

I flung the towel in his face and kicked his feet out from under him. He went into the pool with a shout and a splash. Wilhelmina and I followed him.

Evidently, he didn't like water. He began to thrash, trying to get out. I took him down, right to the bottom. He was a powerhouse but out of his element. I got one arm around his neck and Wilhelmina's snout between his shoulder blades.

I lifted my head clear as I fired, not wanting the effects of underwater concussion. The sound was somewhat muffled, like a heavy cough. In his death agony, Herman's buddy churned the water as though another victim of Jaws.

I knew one thing: Whoever had been on the listening end of the blast must be doing a little churning too, eardrums in shreds. That was one bug that would bug no more.

The unusual sounds had naturally aroused the two legitimate bathers.

"Evidently they like to play games," I said as I climbed out of the pool for the second time. "It takes all kinds."

"But what was that! That explosion!"

"You'll have to ask them. Maybe we need more steam, *jah?*"

Knowing how run a political mileage was tanacod r

CHAPTER 8

Anyone who knows Europe knows how quickly the weather can change. This is particularly true of Berlin. By the time I'd alerted Wehner from a public phone that our conversation had been bugged and requested that Lola and von Winter be put under close surveillance but not brought in for questioning, the sky had clouded over and a chill wind had come up.

By the time I reached the Osdorf, it was beginning to rain. Waiting for me was a priority-1 communication from Hawk. It was in the form of an open telex from AP&WS, telling me to get an interview with West Berlin's Mayor, Klaus Schutes.

Decoded, it said: "Plans changed. President's visit to WB to be announced 17th. President scheduled to arrive Templehof 1000 hrs 18th. Departs for Brussels 1630 18th."

I decided my response would depend on what my meeting with Lutz produced. My reaction at the moment was to signal that the visit be canceled. But I had no way of knowing how much political mileage was expected to be gained by the stopoff. From where I sat, damn little, but then, I didn't sit in the oval office. To me it looked like a phony public-relations appearance during a Communist propaganda brouhaha to prove that *détente*, though still alive and well, didn't mean we were giving up on Berlin. Behind it I saw someone setting the President up for the kill.

I didn't think it was a terrorist gang, like the Baeder-Meinhoff bunch. Assassination and kidnapping were their bag, all right, but they lacked the numbers and the sophistication to carry out an operation that would need a lot of depth. The moves so far indicated depth. Wehner had said, "I don't know what your game is, Nick, but it sounds like the opposition is awfully anxious about you."

It was, but what opposition? On the surface, the KGB had nothing to gain if a presidential assassination could be traced to the Kremlin, and that went for their satellites' espionage agencies as well.

The question arose: what would be the global effect politically and psychologically if a U.S. President, while visiting the bastion of Western resistance to Communism at the height of an East-West peace splurge, was executed by a fellow American—an Oswald, a Ray, a Berger, a Fromme?

N12 had been indicating assassination, Soviet planned, because "blood-wet affairs" came out of the KGB's thirteenth directorate. It wasn't hard to see how the two could fit, providing the KGB's hand remained hidden.

I wasn't optimistic, but there was a chance that what Lutz knew would be enough to give me a leg up on it. Meantime, if Hawk could ferret out who was calling the shots from Washington—someone close enough to the oval office to know when the Berlin idea had come up, or even whoever had suggested it—the back of my neck would feel better.

Before I left the hotel I sent a cable to my cousin John, suggesting he might want to meet me in London on the eighteenth. Translated, it confirmed our original supposition of a deep-cover agent in the White House or on the NSC and said to stand by for a green or red on the President's stop. I could see Hawk scowling over my failure to say when.

It had turned into a lousy, wet, windblown evening. Traffic moved slowly in the rain, and I was in a hurry. Under any other circumstances, Lutz's address would have been laughable. Zimmerstrasse is the narrow, little-used street paralleling the Wall between Friedrichstrasse and Checkpoint Charlie and Stresemann, a major artery. Along it are rows of deteriorating three- and four-story buildings, once quite fashionable. Because of the Wall the real estate of Zimmerstrasse isn't exactly choice. A great many Turkish, Kurdish, and assorted refugees occupy most of the buildings, some profitably involved in East-West drug trade. The police do the best they can.

There are no street lights. What illumination there is comes from the lit-up mine-field area on the other side of the Wall, so the street, which is cobbled and full of refuse, is always in shadow and, on a rainy night, damned deceptive.

I had made my approach to number 18, moving toward Friedrichstrasse, which was lit up like RFK Stadium. There was no chance for concealment. It was just a straight push down a narrow, nasty lane. The building fronts were shuttered. I was fair game for anyone and fairly annoyed at Lutz for having to pick such a meeting place when a zillion others would have been much cleaner, from my point of view. But this, no doubt, was where he lived, and from his point of view, it was safest. But why the hell a former Vopo would want to take up residence within spitting distance of his former guard post, was a question I planned to ask him.

Number 18 was, believe it or not, the corner building. Four stories tall, its side looked out on the allied checkpoint, the big review stand that overlooked the Wall, and the museum. I decided with all the care I'd taken to reach the place, I'd better get in out of the wet before a police patrol came around the corner and asked me for my ID.

It didn't take a genuis to know that Lutz, frightened as he was, believed his safety lay in holing up in his own fort. What caused his fear might be the obvious—or it could be that he was already under the gun, and I was walking into a trap.

The rain spat in my face and the wind huffed around the corner as I eased out the key that Lutz had wrapped in his message. There were big double doors, with an old-fashioned lock. Whatever its fashion, I saw the key wasn't going to open it. No key could—it had been forced. One door was slightly ajar, the wind trying to get an edge on it.

Wilhelmina and I got an edge on it together. No sound came out. No light. I eased the door open wide enough to get an impression. A high-ceilinged empty foyer. No elevator, wooden stairs going up. Form and substance were clear even in the dull lighting from across the Wall. I entered and shut the door behind me, moving away from a line of fire that would make me a target from the stairs.

The foyer's marble floor was good for silent movement. As I waited for my eyes to adjust, the building did the talking, making its own sounds. None of them were hostile in themselves. The hostility was in what I sensed, not in what I heard. I started up the stairs, realizing that the lower level was vacant, and got past the first landing. I met them on the second flight. They had the advantage in numbers, I in timing. They weren't looking for me. I wasn't surprised to meet them. They were in a hurry. I was moving with caution.

The one in the lead saw my form as I sank down on the stairs. He tried to get his gun up as I slammed the Luger's butt against his kneecap. He screamed in agony, jerking forward. I helped him, and he went over my shoulder in a hell of an ass-over-teakettle plunge. Number Two had a silencer on his weapon. It coughed, and I heard the killing whisper pass my ear as Wilhelmina spoke twice for our side.

Number Two choked on her fare and made a headlong pitch. Even though I was down flat, he nearly took me with him.

The third man was not the staying kind. He literally leaped the flight of stairs to get by me. At the landing he stopped long enough to recover his groaning buddy, whose knee I'd smashed. I could hear them scrabbling in a long stumble down to the landing, the door banging open as they went out into the night. Wilhelmina's victim was a silent black mass below.

No one in the building had reacted to the shots and the racket, indicating that it was empty. The question was, had the noise been heard at the Checkpoint? If it had, I'd have a different kind of company soon.

I moved swiftly. Lutz had his flat on the top floor. It wasn't hard to find, because the door was open and light shone out. I wasn't surprised at what I found, only infuriated. Horst Lutz was newly dead. He lay on the floor in a vast puddle of blood, throat cut. His vacant eyes glittered pleadingly at the ceiling.

The flat was large, covering the entire floor, half of it obviously the museum's warehouse, full of stacked books, pamphlets, cartons, and all manner of equipment. There was no time to look around. Whatever Lutz had wanted to tell me, it wasn't likely he'd left it in writing, but I certainly couldn't ignore the possibility.

There was nothing in his pockets, nothing on his desk, nothing in the flat but the silence of the dead, and outside, wailing—not only of the wind, but of police whistles.

I got the hell out.

CHAPTER 9

"We could bring her in." Wehner broke a long silence.

I finished my coffee and shook my head. "No. She wouldn't know that much."

"What about von Winter?"

"If Winter's her control, they'll sweat more wondering why he hasn't been picked up."

"He could tell me what's behind it, even if you won't." He gave me a tight grin and stubbed out his cigarette.

"I don't know either, Paul. One of our people disappeared. I've come looking for him, and three attempts have been made to make me disappear. Lola's contribution was to put the finger on me." We both chuckled.

I sat back in the padded oak chair while Wehner signaled the red-coated waiter for brandy. We had dined well at his private club, no typical German beer hall but a well-appointed *gasthaus* with a select and finely honed membership.

"You understand my willingness to cooperate, Nick,

but I have to give answers too. The helicopter, for example."

He paused, giving the waiter instructions, and I thought about the carpet I'd put him on: *See here, Wehner, who is this American? A helicopter shot out of the sky! The owners are screaming bloody murder. The press is asking questions about the missing passenger. . . .*

"Look," I said, "are you in a jam?"

"Things can get uncomfortable. If I could say something to quiet the Nervous Nellies, to report that I have no explanation, well. . . ." He shrugged. "Would you like a cigar?"

"No, thanks. I'm addicted to these." I took out a gold tip and lit it. "Paul, the record shows that on a particular occasion I was of service to your organization. At that time I did you a favor."

"Yeah, like saving my life."

"That isn't what I meant, but that's on the record too. So your explanation goes like this: I asked for a return favor on the strength of the record, no questions asked— a ride in a helicopter. I haven't a clue who tried to zap me, and as for my reason for wanting a ride, I suggest it be put to Allied Headquarters Command in Heidelberg. If that doesn't bog the whole thing down in paperwork for a year, nothing will."

For the first time since we had sat down, Wehner let go with a bark of his deep gut laughter. "You make it sound easy."

"You know as well as I, that if you want to strangle something in red tape, refer it to higher headquarters, particularly if it's Allied."

"Okay, so maybe I get off the hook, as you say, officially, but Nick, what about unofficially? I'm BND. You're DIA, or whatever. We cooperate, *jah,* but I don't want my service looking like the fellow who is left out in the cold. *Verstehen Sie?"*

Aside from Lola's act and her connection with von Winter, I'd told him nothing. Nor did I intend to. His need to know would be based on developments. Until then—"It's all out in the cold right now. Did you have any luck with the address I gave you?"

He puffed on his cigar and sighed. "It's all tricks, isn't it? I think I'm getting too old for it. Nothing is simple any more, and nothing is what it seems. At 2200 hours you will have a visitor at your hotel, a *fraulein*. She is an instructor at the university. She will tell you about the address. Believe me, she is not one of ours, not BND, not an agent for anyone."

"I don't get it."

"You will."

"And then after I see her, you will. Is that the idea?"

He sighed again, and in the subdued light he suddenly looked older, frayed around the edges. "Perhaps, perhaps not. She'll make the decision. If you could tell me where you got the address, it might help."

I sat there, staring at my brandy glass, concealing my annoyance. What kind of silly-assed game was this? This wasn't Paul Wehner. This wasn't the pro I'd known, who operated, got answers, didn't ask fool questions and then come up with muddy nonsense about schoolteachers making decisions.

"It's all fucked up!" he said, disgust and anger in the rumble of his voice. "Once you had a job, *jah*. You knew where you stood, even if you didn't know why, and you knew that whatever happened, you'd get support. Now some damn faceless eunuch in Bonn gets a bright idea on how we can kiss their asses over there, and that makes everybody think it's all sugar candy!" He filled his schnapps glass for the sixth time. "Look, Nick, go along and see this girl."

"What's her name? Where does she fit in?"

"Hilma Raeder. Listen to what she has to say, and then we'll talk again, *jah*? That's as much as I can do now. I'm under orders."

I had two choices. I could break contact and go my own way, which was my usual style, or I could play along and see what Hilma had to say. The trouble with the first choice was that West German Intelligence would be on my tail immediately, at best a hindrance, at worst, an adversary. It looked as if Wehner was caught in the middle and nobody really knew what the hell was going on.

"How are things in the morgue?" I said, wanting time to think.

"We can pay a visit. . . . Nick, I'm sorry about all this." He looked unhappy, contrite, a little drunk.

"Paul, it was a helluva good meal. I appreciate all you've done. I know you're in a bind, officially. We'll play it by ear, okay?"

His face brightened a bit. "Okay."

"Let's go cheer up the boys in the morgue."

There was damn little cheer. Klaus Kraemer's body had been burned beyond normal recognition. During the war, as a small boy, he'd taken a bomb splinter in the skull. It had been a large one, and a metal patch had been used to plug the gap.

When AXE had taken him on an additional identification check was added to his file. A minor operation was performed, the plate exposed, and the letter *K* engraved on it. Blackened as the metal was, the *K* stood out. Not unusual for Berlin or Germany.

Now that Lutz was also dead, Kraemer had left no next of kin to claim his body. However, the police would have been reluctant to release it for burial because the victim had died, not by fire, but from three gunshot wounds from a heavy-caliber automatic, probably a Mauser. The police report showed no witnesses to the shooting and no explanation for the fire, but indicated both could have been the result of robbery. The fire had been detected at 0320, two days earlier.

"Is he the man you're looking for?" Wehner's question annoyed me. He knew better than to ask it in front a police sergeant. He knew better than to ask it at all.

to the curb I hit the accelerator and swung hard. On the slick street the DL244 slewed around in a 180, as I tapped the brake to speed the action. Then, head low, I went back up Leibnizstrasse full bore.

I heard the snap, crackle and pop of shattered glass, flakes of it showering me. I slewed left into a side street near the end of the block and kept right on coming around, bouncing off the curb, shifting down, cornering, so that I shot back into Leibnizstrasse, heading back where I'd come from.

The black Maria had backed out of the entrance drive and was pulling away. I had the window down and Wilhelmina in hand, but someone was playing tail-ass Charlie. They saw me coming and went barreling away. I could have startled a lot of pigeons and shaken up the peace planners, but it was no contest. The black job went around a corner and was out of sight before I reached the hotel.

I thought I'd better concentrate on Zitor's condition. He had a nasty lump on the head and an equally bruised ego. He did not like being coldcocked on his own home ground. He didn't have much to say, but I had the feeling he wanted to blame me for his own carelessness. When I showed him the punctured Volvo, he grunted.

There were two messages for me. One was from Lola, asking that I call, and the other was from my editor, Hawk, requesting a telephone conversation regarding the quality of the copy I was filing. He would expect to hear from me at midnight GMT.

It was five minutes to ten when the phone buzzed and the heavy-voiced clerk behind the reception desk announced the arrival of Fraulein Raeder.

Hilma Raeder was no whey-faced searcher for intellectual enlightenment, nor was she a dungareed, unwashed, pot-smoking freak. Slavic ancestry showed in her high cheekbones, and there was a slightly Oriental cast to her very direct brown eyes. She had a firm mouth with a nicely curled underlip, a solid chin, and an upturned nose.

Her skin had a honey tone that went with her light brown hair. Hilma Raeder was no beauty queen, but in face and figure she radiated a quiet magnetism that was damned attractive. The way she said, "Mr. Carter?" in English was an added touch. It went with the husky quality of her voice.

"A bad night," I replied, in English also, taking her raincoat, observing the good taste in her expensive pant-suit. Hilma knew how to count her *phennigs*. "I'm sorry you had to come out in it."

"Herr Wehner said I could trust you." She got right to the point, serious and tense.

"Why don't we sit here?" I said, indicating the circular table.

She took in the outer room of the suite, noticed the door to the bedroom was closed. "We are alone, sir?"

"Yes. As a newsman, Fraulein, I don't like sharing my stories. I have coffee or a drink. Which would you prefer?"

She hesitated a moment, her eyes skittery. Then she sighed. "All right. Coffee, thanks." She took off her yellow rain hat and shook her hair free.

I poured the coffee while she sat down. "Cigarette?"

"No, I don't smoke. I'll take it black, thanks."

"Spoken like a true sailor."

"Berlin has other sports to occupy it."

I set the cup before her and sat down. "Okay, Fraulein Raeder," I said, matching her mood and tone, "what can I do for you?"

"Tell me where you got that address you gave Herr Wehner."

"Why?"

"Because it's terribly important to know."

"To whom?"

"I can't say, only that lives depend on it."

"Herr Wehner said you can trust me. We both know his business. You know mine. What's yours?"

"I teach art history at—"

"Which has nothing to do with the history we have here. Nothing to do with your question—or the obvious seriousness behind it."

Her face was set. She was having trouble keeping calm. "You said you are a journalist, Herr Carter. An American." There was a note of distaste in the last.

"You trust Paul, obviously. You are here because—"

"Because I am desperate. I must have your answer." She had her fists clenched on either side of the cup.

"You'll get it when you tell me what it's all about. Wehner knows I'll print nothing you tell me, even if I am an American." That added some color to her cheeks. "Otherwise, he wouldn't have sent you, would he?"

She stared at me a moment, then sat back with a sigh and shook her head. "I don't know."

"I don't know either. But I do know the only way we're going to get anywhere, Fraulein, is to take the chance of trusting each other."

"Chance!" she scoffed. "Where is there any chance for you!"

"There's blood on that address, some of it nearly mine."

That stiffened her for a moment. Her eyes fell away as she picked up her cup and sipped at it. She had a nice clean scent. She wore little makeup, and her fingernails were natural and unpolished.

"Herr Carter"—she put down her cup, mind made up, eyes glinting—"if you should write this story or tell anyone—if any of it gets out, I—I swear I'll have you shot."

"I'll take the risk, if you will." I smiled faintly, not being sarcastic but letting her know that I took her seriously.

"All right. Tell me, and I'll tell you."

I shook my head. "I'm from the old unliberated school. Ladies first."

"I could shoot you right now." She meant every word of it.

"Which would do neither of us any good. Have some more coffee." I poured while she calmed down.

She took a deep breath. "Do you know what an escape helper refers to?"

"No," I lied. "I assume it means what it says."

"When the Wall went up, students at the university formed secret groups to help their families and friends to get out—to get here to the Western zone. They were called escape helpers."

"Sure. I remember. That was way back when . . . long before your time."

She gave me a cold look. "It was all volunteer work. Digging tunnels, using tricked-up automobiles. Some of the escape helpers got killed. Then in 1968 the government passed a law forbidding us to continue the work. It caused a lot of protest, a lot of trouble."

"As I recall there was a lot of student trouble in those days, and it didn't have anything to do with freeing people in the East." I let my skepticism hang out.

"That's right. There were many who thought having the same politics, like being against Vietnam, would help bring the Wall down. Up until 1971 most students gave up the idea of working on escapes."

"So what started it up again?"

"The new accord on Berlin. It permits us thirty days of visiting a year in the East. That made it easier to plan escapes. But most of the people who did the planning did it as a business. They charged a lot of money."

"Yes, I know. I did a couple of stories on it."

"It made the authorities here furious, and on the other side they shouted their propaganda, saying see, they're so decadent over there they have to be paid for everything. They even said the West Berlin government was making money out of it."

"Yeah, when all the time Bonn was forking out millions of marks to buy people out of the East. I've written on that, too."

She tucked her head down. "Don't make fun, Herr

Carter. You don't live here in Berlin. You don't understand a thing about it."

"I'm dead serious. It's true, isn't it?"

She looked up at me, her eyes glacial. "It's true they try to buy back the children who have been separated from their parents who have managed to get here."

"Okay. So what are we getting at?"

"The Free University meant just that once. Last year when it held its twentieth anniversary, the student body forced the faculty to honor the occasion in the city museum, while it celebrated by inviting a Soviet dance group to be featured on the campus."

"Peace in our time, yes?"

Her eyes remained locked on mine. "At that time a few of us got together and wondered if there was anything we could do. Anything that would draw attention to us again as an important place of freedom, where young people could be seen as ready to take a risk to prove it and to show that beyond that damned Wall and that hypocritical Helsinki Treaty, those people in power over there are no different than—than Hitler!"

I was swiftly cultivating a genuine love for Fraulein Hilma Raeder—a rarity! An honest-to-God idealistic virgin in a cesspool of political rape artists!

"What are you smiling at!" she snapped angrily, her color rising again.

"Go on," I said. "I'm on your side."

She stared at me, then relaxed a bit. "Well, there are eight of us in it. I'm the only woman. In the old days they used to dig tunnels. Tunnels are old-fashioned." She stopped and looked at her cup.

"And you're old-fashioned," I said.

Her head jerked up, her eyes narrowed. "How do you know that?"

"An educated guess. How long have you been at it?"

"Over a year."

"How come their detection equipment hasn't picked up your tunneling?"

"We've gone very deep. And right under their noses, you might say."

"How close are you to finishing?"

"Very close." It was eye-locking time again.

"And when you come up?"

"When we come up, we bring out forty-eight men, women, and children, and we show them to all Berlin and to all the world, and we show them that freedom is not something you buy back and forth!" Her voice had risen.

"How come forty-eight?"

My practical question stumped her for a second. "Our plan has been for each to select six relatives or friends. Each group is unknown to the others, and only one of us knows the identity of all."

I could see it coming a mile away, and I was beginning to feel sad. "And why is the address I gave Herr Wehner so important?"

"Herr Carter, it is the address in the Eastern zone where the escape will be made from. How did you get it?"

I lit one of my gold tips while she sat like a coiled spring. "Where does Wehner fit into it?"

"He's well-known to one of our members. We decided at the beginning to keep him somewhat informed so that if anything happened to us, the authorities would be prepared to act in whatever way they saw fit."

What Hilma and her friends were up to sounded like amateur night. But her explanation of Paul's part in the mole goal had the tangy odor of a ripe Brie left on the stove. In view of all else, BND had to have a fairly good reason for playing along, since what these babes in the digging business were up to was absolutely *verboten*. But letting them commit suicide was hardly in keeping with *détente* or *Ostpolitik* . . . unless the plan was to arrest them all at the last minute.

"Where did you get the address, *bitte?*" Hilma's voice had a nice grate.

"I'll make a deal with you," I said. "Show me where you're digging the tunnel and give me an exclusive on when the escape will take place, and I'll answer your question."

She swore at me—in German, but in any language her meaning was clear. "You damned American swine!" Her eyes blazed, breasts outthrust.

"Look at it from my position," I said. "I tell you what you want to know. You leave. I never see you again until I read about the escape in *Die Welt*. I'm a newspaper man, honey. This is a great story, and like Wehner said—you can trust me."

It took a bit of time for her to get her composure back. "I-I have the feeling this is all some kind of joke to you. All you care about is your story, not the risk, not the lives, not the meaning."

"The meaning is copy, Hilma. That's what my editor pays me for. I think what you're doing is right on. All I want to see is where you're doing it."

"You mean you don't believe me!" Her fists were doubled again.

"I believe every single word. That's why I want to see where. What do you say we go?"

"I could shoot you," she said, standing up.

"Like I said, that wouldn't do either of us any good. I'll call a taxi."

"A taxi! You are a bloody fool! We'll go in my car."

CHAPTER 11

Her car was a VW, of course, parked right in front of the hotel. Sitting in it were two very large Teutonic knights. She spoke to them quickly in German. "We will have to take him." They didn't argue. They didn't say anything. They sized me up as I climbed in the back. The flowing-haired blond drove. His name was Tostig. My equally blond rear-seat companion was Dieter.

The first indication that there might be a grain of professionalism in the operation was the route Tostig followed. It covered half of downtown, a five-kilo jaunt, going through the Tiergarten, a couple of swings around the radio tower, and then some back-street twisting until we came out in Schoneberg, where we parked.

No one had said a word. Hilma swung her head to face me. "We walk to the S-Bahn now. Just do as you're told."

"Sure we weren't followed?" I said.

She didn't bother to reply.

Fifteen minutes later, after we had changed trains three times, we came back down to the street. I had come to realize that this part of the demonstration was not to throw off possible pursuit, but to confuse me on our location. It didn't confuse me, but it surprised me a bit. We weren't far from Checkpoint Charlie and Friedrichstrasse.

"I'll go ahead," she told the men in German. "Bring him in ten minutes."

"I don't like it," Tostig growled.

"Nor I," Dieter seconded.

"Right now there's no choice." She turned, rain hat pulled down, coat collar turned up, and walked away from us, going down a narrow side street.

The three of us stood under the shelter of the S-Bahn overhang. The rain was at it again.

"Cigarette?" I produced mine.

They grunted negatively. I lit up, thinking about Hilma. She'd gone down a street that would end at the Wall. If my sense of direction was on target she'd come out on Zimmerstrasse. If my sense of smell was as accurate, the stink was getting worse.

"Ve go," said Tostig, nodding.

Ve vent, following in Hilma's wet footsteps. We had walked a short block before Tostig, who was leading the way through the murk of the unlighted street, called a halt.

He turned and faced me. "Ve black the eyes now, *jah?*" He raised his hands to his eyes, and Dieter, who was behind me, covered my eyes with a blindfold.

"Ve make very quiet," Dieter muttered.

I was willing to play along until the specifics got straightened out. Each got an arm and guided me. Their strength communicated itself through their fingers. George Allen could certainly have used them up front.

We went across the street and around a corner, across the street again, and into what I judged to be an alley, where we kicked a few cans and came to a halt.

Hilma whispered in German, "All right, bring him in," and then to me, "Watch the step."

I watched the step. There were one up and a dozen go-

ing down. The back basement entrance, I figured. The
rain had stopped and the damp mustiness of an empty
building hit my nostrils. A short distance farther, Hilma
again warned me to watch my step.

We descended again, this time six steps; then I was
warned to keep my head down. Blindman's buff went on
for quite a time. Through a built-in and carefully trained
sense of direction, I knew we had passed through the cellar basements of at least three buildings, following the
same general course. Finally, we went down a last flight, a
makeshift set of steps, and came to a halt. I could hear a
cranking sound and smell the heavy smell of damp earth.

The blindfold was removed, and I blinked in the dull
light, taking in the surroundings. They weren't much, but
they said a lot for the excavating ability of the tunnel diggers. We were standing in a narrow open space with lum-
ber piled on either side, and beyond it, in every direction
but one, earth had been piled up almost to ceiling level.
The weak light came from a chain of bulbs that disappeared into the tunnel entrance. A passageway behind me
had led to the digs, and a passageway that branched off to
the right toward the cellar wall had been opened up. But
the real point of serious interest was the tunnel entrance
in front of us. Beside it were two hefty academicians
dressed in shorts, cranking on a handle attached to a
smartly rigged drum, winding up a wire running down
into the tunnel, whose entrance shelved sharply. They
sure as hell got A for construction and muscle power.

"Too bad you don't have a couple of mules," I said.

Dieter and Tostig had taken off their coats and gone to
relieve their buddies. Hilma was speaking quickly and
quietly to the other two, explaining. They came toward
me, smelling of sweat and dirt.

"I am Jan. He is Peter," Jan said in good English. "You
will tell Fraulein Raeder what she wants to know. *Jah?*"
He was a bit older than the others, dark and finely built,
handsome, with very direct brown eyes.

"The tunnel between the outhouse and the bakery on Bernauerstrasse was 145 meters. Is yours longer?"

"You know a lot about such things, hey?" Jan wiped his mouth with the back of his arm.

"Why wouldn't I? I'm a newspaperman." I turned to Hilma. "Will you let me see what you've done?"

The drum winders had brought into view a dirt-loaded cart with rubber tires.

"Where did you get the address?" Hilma said. "We want to know right now."

"Hadn't we better dump that first?" I said, thinking that the Bernauer tunnel had been dug by thirty-six diggers, while these young mining experts numbered only eight.

"We'll dump you, unless you speak as she says," Jan said.

As he threatened, I saw Dieter pick up a phone receiver by the tunnel entrance and speak a few words.

"All right," I said. "Horst Lutz gave it to me."

I expected the reaction. Dead silence. Shock. I could see Hilma's eyes wide and glittering, staring at me in disbelief. "I don't believe it!" she choked.

"I'm sorry, but it's so." I dropped the hotshot newsman role.

"How? Why?"

"At the museum at Checkpoint Charlie. I went there to see Hildebrandt, the director. Lutz was there. I'd written a piece about him after his escape. I guess he recognized me. I could tell he was upset. He passed me the address and Paul Wehner's name. When I tried to talk to him he got busy with a group of tourists, and I knew he either couldn't or didn't want to talk. I've known Paul Wehner for a long time. I figured Lutz wanted me to give him the address. So now you know what I know."

We stood in a huddle, Hilma explaining in German what I had just told her. They were all badly shaken, and it was obvious why. Lutz was one of their group. The address was the point of escape—the *eingang*—from the

other side. I was beginning to see some light in the half
darkness. It was time to stop playing along for the ride.

"Lutz was one of you, wasn't he?"

"That's none of your business!" Jan snapped.

Hilma sighed and looked away.

"I've got very bad news for you," I said, and told them
the very bad news. Before I'd finished, Hilma had her
hands up to her face, choking back the tears.

Jan translated harshly to his pals. Then he faced me.
"How did you know to go to Zimmerstrasse?" It was a
growl.

"He gave me that address too and the time to meet
him. I got there too late."

"If what you say makes true, you're lucky. You get
there sooner, you be dead now."

Hilma took her hands down from her face. "We have
been betrayed," she said in German. "We have got to
stop."

"Who would want to kill Horst?" Jan asked, looking
down the side passage to the hole in the cellar wall.

The eyes of the others followed his, and I got the
message. Lutz had lived in the house next door. The hole
was the connection.

"Don't ask stupid questions!" Hilma's voice cracked in
anger and grief. "Horst had all the names, the photographs."

A bell clanged. "You mean of those who are
escaping?" I said in German.

"You speak German!" Hilma gasped.

"What of it?" I snapped. The time for fun and games
was over. Photographs were the answer. Lutz had shown
them to his uncle. Kraemer had seen something that worried him. He'd asked for Sparks, and N12 had recognized
someone and sent his message. The someone was obviously an assassin, maybe more than one. Cute. Hilma was
right; they had been betrayed—right from the start.

"I don't think whoever killed Lutz found anything."

"How do you know that?" It was all in German now.

"From what I saw, the place wasn't torn up. He may have surprised whoever broke in."

"We've got to warn them," Jan said. "There can be no attempt made now."

"You may be jumping to conclusions, if—"

"Listen, you, you stay the hell out of this!" Jan took a step toward me.

"Calm down, buddy. If it weren't for me, you could all end up in Karlshorst about the time you stopped digging."

Jan wasn't listening. He swung with his right. I caught his wrist and elbow, reversed, and flung him. He hit on his back with a heavy thunk, and I was glad the piled earth was soft.

"Like I said, calm down." I faced the others, and for a second I thought we were all going to get dirty.

Then Hilma ordered sharply, "Stop it! Stop it! He's right!" And then, more in control, "I want to hear what he has to say."

Jan was on his feet, breathing heavily, eager to even the score.

"Jan," I said, "I'm sorry. You and I getting dirty won't help. If you want to try it again later, okay."

Hilma grabbed his arm. "Jan, you just stop it!"

It was a good thing she was there. Against the four of them, I'd have had it rough.

Hilma stood between Jan and me. "Now what do you have to say, Herr Carter! Everything you've had to say so far has been bad."

"It could go something like this. East Berlin security has had its eye on Lutz. After all, he's been a Vopo, and he flaunts it by working at the museum. They got suspicious of him. He realized it and when he recognized me this morning, he passed me the address."

"Why would he do that?" Dieter asked.

"That's what I'd hoped to find out."

"Why not contact one of us instead?" Tostig got in his oar.

"Because if he knew he was under suspicion he wouldn't want to expose us," Hilma answered.

"He knew Wehner and I were old press friends," I said. "Wehner had introduced us right after his escape so I could do the story on him. He knew I'd pass the address on to Paul."

"But it's got to mean they know what we're doing." She looked toward the tunnel entrance.

"Certainly it's possible, but why go to all the trouble of killing Lutz and alerting you when all they have to do is wait until the escape is to take place? Incidently, when is the escape date?"

"That's something you don't have to know," Jan said.

"My suggestion," I told Hilma, "is that whenever it is, you cancel it for a week. That will at least buy you some time."

"Time for what?" snapped Jan.

"Oh, Jan, stop it! Can't you see he's trying to help?"

Jan turned away, brushing some of the dirt he'd picked up off his back.

"How can we send a signal now?" Tostig said.

Peter spoke for the first time. "None of us can risk going over there."

"Don't you have a mail code?"

"No, mail is too risky," Hilma answered. "We have a daily meeting place set up in case there is a need for contact. We make it by a telephone call to a party on the other side, my aunt. My uncle, Jan Steuben, is the escape director from there. He will make the arrangements."

"Okay, you make the call. I'll be your contact. No one suspects me of anything, but Jan, here."

I grinned at him, and after a second Dieter punched his arm and they all managed a rueful chuckle. They were an okay bunch, but they were going to end up like their pal Horst, if I didn't get moving.

new he was under, suspicion he

CHAPTER 12

I granted Wehner's wish. I called him from a kiosk. I let him say, "Wehner speaking," and then I lit into him.

"Will you tell me what in the name of hell you people think you're doing? That exercise is a beautiful job of earth moving, but just who do you think they're kidding? You'd better make it good!"

"Jah, but not on the phone."

"On the phone you tell me quick: When is the flag due to go up?"

"Maybe Wednesday, but—"

"Either you'll stop it or I will. In one sentence tell me why you've played along."

"Because if it worked it would show something!" His voice rose.

"If it worked, my arse! And if it didn't work?"

"It would show the same damn thing! Everyone would know!"

"You mean Bonn approved this?"

"Never mind that! You come to my place and—"

79

"You silly bastard!" I hung up.

In spite of the CIA's disembowelment, there are still Agency safe houses in West Berlin where an AXE agent can check in with the correct code word of the day and stay low. In such a house I lay on my bed blowing smoke rings, slinging my thoughts through them like darts.

First Paul Wehner. His behavior, particularly at dinner, had become clear. He was treading on very thin ice—was way out of bounds, his neck on the block. The official policy of the BND as reflected by the official policy of the Bonn government was to take direct action against any freelance attempts by freedom lovers in the West to help those in the East who wanted to get out. It had been so since Willy Brandt had begun his opening to the East in '69—his *Ostpolitik*.

Now, on his own, a BND station chief was permitting such an attempt. Obviously he didn't know all the details and didn't want to. But he'd known Horst Lutz, and through him he'd set me up with Hilma. The question was, why hadn't he set me up with Lutz? Supposedly he was going along with the plan because whatever happened, the attempt was going to attract attention to West Berlin at the height of a *détente* blast. He wanted me to think that the frustration of having to carry out his government's policy had got to him, that he'd gone over the hill and was no longer a reliable security agent. By the rules of the game he'd become a rogue elephant. That could be true, or else he was playing some other kind of game.

The phone buzzed, and I knew my call to Hawk had come through. I filled him in quickly and then waited for the scrambler to do its unscrambling. I could practically smell the brimstone from his special brand of parboiled cheroot.

"Kinda smells, doesn't it?" He didn't mean the smoke. "The timing is cute, but calling the delay should make the thing a side issue. The President will be long gone. The whole thing could be a diversion, Nick."

"I realize that, sir, but both Kraemer and Lutz are dead, N12 is probably dead, and somebody is awfully anxious to have me join them. The only connection we have is the tunnel."

"Yes, and who led you to it?"

"But Wehner doesn't know about the planned visit, and if he did, why would he expose himself as he has? If I called Bonn, he'd be out in the snow."

"You have a point. If the MFS knows about the tunnel, what was the point in killing Lutz?"

"You mean you think the killings have to do with something else. If that was so, what was N12 doing writing down the escape address?"

"Don't ask me to do your job. I'm suggesting alternatives."

"I'm considering them, sir, but I have to go on what I've got. Lutz's message to me could only mean what N12 wrote. It is barely possible that the MFS is not on to the tunnel, but they're on to something else that's close to it. I haven't figured out what, but I'm working on it."

"Don't have much time, do you?" he cracked, and I could see the sardonic squint. "What about the photographs of the forty-eight who are coming out?"

"Lutz had them. If the MFS knows about the plan, they have them too. I'm going back to Zimmerstrasse and see what I can find."

"Well, whatever you find, there's only one question here—should the President cancel? Unless I have something solid, I can't recommend it. State feels there's a lot of political mileage to be gained, so does the NSC."

"Anyone in particular?"

"That's being worked on. Nick, I need a go, no-go from you by Monday at the latest. The other agencies feel there's no more risk than the normal, and they're taking all measures."

"Does Bonn know yet?"

"Not till Monday, not till I hear from you."

Inwardly I gave a sigh of relief. If Bonn had been clued

in, then Wehner would have known, and that would have meant what I was beginning to suspect, that he had gone over and was a double. "I'll keep in touch," I said.

"Do that, son. And stay well."

CHAPTER 13

Today it's no problem for the tourist to enter East Berlin. There are two principal openings through the Wall, at Checkpoint Charlie and the Friedrichstrasse U-Bahn station. I chose the former, not only because that was the route the tour bus followed, but also because the bus parked across the street, on Unter den Linden, from the Karl Marx platz, the open-air café where the contact was to be made. The stop was made so that before going back to West Berlin, the sightseers could spend the remainder of their East marks on coffee and pastry. A part of the clearance ceremony before being permitted into the Communist zone was to exchange West marks for East on a one-to-one basis, when the actual value was about four to one. That way the DDR got you coming and going, a kind of Marxist capitalist ripoff.

The bus, East German owned and operated, had an ersatz Wagnerian girl guide full of sweetness and light. Beneath the veneer, MFS was stamped all over the ass of her size-sixteen dark blue uniform and her very observant myopic eyes.

When the bus had passed Zimmerstrasse on the way east, she was explaining that "pazzphorts vill need to be hexamined," but she didn't miss the West German police car parked in front of the late Horst Lutz's address.

I figured if the police did a thorough job and had a look at the building's cellar, they'd spot the hole in the wall, leading to the tunnel digs, and the need for my journey would be wasted.

Actually, the method of contact was not bad, for amateurs. The café, like so many of the new buildings along Unter den Linden and the Alexanderplatz, had a double purpose: to indicate East German prosperity and to make it clear that it is East Berlin that is a capital city and not West Berlin. The outside patio of the café was a large marble expanse with a center fountain and tables all about. The prices were low; the coffee, orange squash, and beer, not bad.

The contact was to be made without contact. I was carrying a copy of *Neus Deutchland*, the official East German newspaper, in my left hand. Sticking out of the right pocket of my jacket was a tourist map of Berlin. The time of contact, if one was to be made, was between 1400 and 1500 hours. The particular bus made its scheduled stop at 1445, and that was why I had selected it.

Our Brunhilda had informed us that we had twenty minutes to enjoy East German beverages or Russian vodka. Some of the passengers tittered in expectation. Then they hustled and bustled across the street and up the marble steps.

The contact plan was simple and safe enough. When I had left Hilma and her diggers, she had called her aunt in East Berlin and, in the course of the conversation, had said she was hoping to make a visit soon. (Hilma's uncle,

Jan Steuben, the key man in the operation on that side, would set up the contact). That was the signal, and her Uncle Jan would take it from there.

At this hour there were supposed to be many empty tables, which was one reason for selecting this time. However, Hilma hadn't taken into account the youth forum, and things were pretty well filled up. The tables were numbered, and mine, number twenty-seven, was occupied by a scruffy-looking couple. The contact was to be at number twenty-eight. It was occupied by a middle-aged man, his frau, and two young boys. The man's back was to me. The couple could be Hilma's uncle and aunt, with the boys along to add to the normalcy of the scene.

I reached my table, and the male occupant, with unwashed looks and scraggly goatee, looked up from his equally attractive bag and said in low German, "This table is in use."

"That's right," I said, and sat down.

"You are not invited!" he snarled angrily, leaning forward so that I got the stink of him. "This is private!"

"Nothing is private in the DDR," I said. "We all share equally. But I'm going to share some private information with you both. You need a bath. Either go someplace and get one, or I'll throw you in that fountain."

They stared at me, not sure what or who I was, and then we all looked up as the tour guide, Fraulein Ludmilla, came to stand beside us. *"Bitte, mein Herr,* may I join?"

I rose. "But, of course, Fraulein, you may join. My pleasure." I moved to hold her chair, and as she sat down the couple got up and went off, muttering, seeking their fetid privacy.

"Well," she said, ignoring their departure, "have you enjoyed the tour?"

"Top drawer." I smiled. "The bus is very comfortable too."

She looked puzzled, her inflated breasts seeking some

way out of their confinement. *"Bitte,* if you will excuse, what is top drawer?"

"Everything seemed to go very well, first rate, if you know what I mean."

"Ahh!" She nodded. "I zeee!

While she was zeeing, I offered her a cigarette. *"Ach,* it is not permitted while on duty." And then she got down to business. "You know, *mein Herr,* if you will excuse again, you do not seem like the others."

"No? Why's that?"

"The way you look, not like a tourist."

I laughed. "Well, that's nice. You don't look like a tour guide either. But what do I look like to you, a spy maybe?" I grinned. "All the notes I've been taking."

That flustered her a bit, "Oh, you make joke."

"Not at all. I think you have a perfect right to be suspicious."

"It's not like a tourist. I mean—"

"But who said I was a tourist, Fraulein?"

"Oh, well, if you pay to take the tour then you must be a tourist."

I had seen the waiter approaching, and I signaled. The method arranged to pass information was in the choice of words in giving the order. I thought it would be nice for Ludmilla to help in the process.

"Mein Herr." The waiter, with stained jacket and a nice proletarian slouch, held his pad at the ready.

"Ask him what he suggests," I said to my visiting girlfriend.

"What do you suggest?" she dutifully asked in German.

The German word *an-deuten,* suggest, meant danger.

"Suggest." He repeated. "To eat or to drink?"

She translated, and I added, "I don't think there will be time to eat."

"Maybe some baked apple?"

"No, no, I just meant to drink. Is there some specialty?"

"Everything is special," she said proudly.

"Well, tell me yours." I looked into her glistening eyes and shuddered at the thought that she might.

"An orange squash, *bitte*."

"All right, ask him for an orange squash and a pilsner."

She gave the order. Pilsner meant, escape delayed.

"And ask him, if you would, does he have any matches."

She asked. The word for matches is *streichholzen,* and the first seven letters stood for seven days. Not bad for college kids.

The order was placed, and Ludmilla got back to me. "So you are not a tourist."

"Nor even a spy."

She snickered. "So, what are you?"

"A dirty, rotten, imperialist journalist who came along to do a story on your tour."

Her round somewhat blotchy face took on an even blotchier hue. "A journalist!" She grew stiff around the gills.

"Yes." I took the newspaper from my pocket and put it on the table. This was both the close-off signal and proof of identity. "Maybe you'd like to tell me what it says."

"*Mein Herr*, journalists must register with the Ministry of Information. It is not permitted to do this!" She wasn't a girl guide any more, but a worried security chick who could be in a jam if I wrote something unfriendly about the tour and identified her.

I patted her clenched fist. "Now, don't you worry about a thing. I have only praise for the fine line of hokum you've been handing out. Really most impressive *détente*-crap."

She relaxed a bit. *"Bitte, was ist, hockfum und ahh, dé-tentecrap?"*

The waiter arrived, put down our drinks, and then

handed the bill to the heavy-shouldered man at the next
table.

"What is the German word for excellent?" I asked,
knowing that when the man at the next table rose he
would see the paper.

CHAPTER 14

Hilma, in tight-fitting dungarees and loose-fitting shirt, wore a worried look. "Your description of the woman sounds like my aunt, and the boys two of my cousins, but the man, I'm not sure." The fading afternoon light, coming in from the large side window of her nicely decorated one-room flat, bathed her face, highlighting her features, giving it a sensuous look.

"Why not?"

"It could have been, but I haven't seen my uncle since I was a little girl, and then I remember him as being not broad, but tall. He's an engineer, and the few times I have gone to the East zone to see my Aunt Gertrude, he has been away on business." She sat on her large day bed, Yoga style, her legs crossed before her, her eyes never leaving mine.

"Let's go back to the beginning. How did you set this thing up in the first place?"

"Each of us contacted one family or one friend. They

89

in turn contacted one other, up to six. We didn't dare make it any larger than that."

"Does your uncle know the identity of those outside his family?"

"He knows the key person in each group."

"How come he was selected as escape director?"

"Horst Lutz knew him, had been his student in a trade course. He knew how solid he was."

"I suppose you latched on to Horst because he was an escaped Vopo."

"Yes, and because he'd been involved in other escapes. We all had the idea that Horst had some kind of official approval, even though we knew it was not officially permitted."

"Wehner?"

"Well, as you know, he is a news editor with the SPD, but we—"

"Do the others in the group know him?"

"No. I don't even know him. I just had heard his name from Horst. He called and gave me the information you had given him and told me where I could find you."

"How many know the escape point?"

She shook her head. "I don't know. That was to be my uncle's decision."

"Then if anything happened to your uncle everything could go up in smoke, either because the others wouldn't know where to go or because the Vopos would be waiting."

She sighed and shook her head again. "We knew it was a chance, but it was the best we could do."

Actually, it wasn't a bad plan, but the dangers in it were obvious. If Uncle Jan was smart, he'd have a backup man, someone he might pass on the street at an appointed time and place with the proper signal. Of course, if the MFS boys had him they'd get everything out of him anyway.

"Do you think they've caught on to it?"

"Would there be any point in killing Horst if they had?"

"If they knew he had the photographs."

"If they know, they don't need any photographs." Although my answer was an obvious conclusion, what she had said jangled a new thought. "Did Horst have the identities of all the escapees as well as their photographs?"

"No, just the photographs for checking when the escape is made."

Well, that answered that, and I'd been awfully slow in picking it up. There wasn't a doubt in the world that the MFS was on to it and had been right from the start.

I turned from the window, and her eyes followed me. "Do you have a diagram of the tunnel?" I wanted to divert her thinking while I clarified my own.

"I can show you." She rose and moved to a corner desk. Her attitude toward me had undergone a decided change. The vibes were good, and as I stood beside her while she unfolded a dogeared map of Berlin, they became even stronger. "Here," she said, pointing to Zimmerstrasse. "And then so." Her arm brushed mine.

The line of the tunnel ran under the minefield and under the control point at an angle, which for brazen ingenuity wasn't bad. On the other side of the control, it made a dogleg and ended at Schutzen just beyond the security zone. Altogether it was one helluva piece of mine work, and no doubt the longest of the dozen escape tunnels that had been dug since the Wall went up in '61.

"Where does it *ausgang?* There are damn few buildings along Schützen, and they're all under security control."

"There's a new café built off the end building. It's for the Vopos, but other workers use it too."

"Nothing like working under the enemy's nose." When she saw I was smiling, she smiled too. "And what time does the party take place?"

"But it is a party! How did you know that!" She looked shaken, and I had trouble taking my eye off her lovely underlip.

"I didn't. It's just a slang expression, like saying, when does the curtain go up?"

"Oh, I see. Well"—she got her eyes back on the map—"they will start coming at twelve-thirty noon. The café will be reserved for a special family reunion at one. It will be closed to everyone except those who are escaping. They will make it look like a real party."

"That sounds pretty slick. How can you set something like that up in the DDR?"

"My uncle. One of his men is to retire. The celebration will be for him. The DDR likes that sort of affair."

I turned away from her, wanting the answer to one more question. N12 had written down the Schützen address when he should have written down Uncle Jan's. That either meant he didn't know it, which was hard to believe, or there was something about the café he'd gone to check on, or he was going there as a point of departure.

"How many in your group knew your uncle's address?"

"Only myself."

I swung around. "Not Horst?"

She shook her head. "No, my uncle moved after Horst escaped."

"And you decided to operate on a need-to-know basis."

"Yes." She was looking at me with an undefinable expression. "Who are you?" Her voice was almost a whisper. "I don't believe you're a newspaperman at all."

"Why do you say that? Of course I am." I moved closer to her.

"No." She shook her head again. I liked the gesture. "You know too much, and now today, someone was following me."

That brought me up short. "Where? When?" I said quietly, raising my finger to my lips.

"When I left my class before coming here." She spoke softly, quickly. "There was a man on the steps, a stranger. I'm a Berliner." Her chin came up. "I know he followed me."

"All the way home?"

"I don't think so. I changed trains very quickly at the Zoo. I didn't see him when I got off."

"How soon did you get here, before I arrived?" I was moving toward the door.

"Maybe ten minutes."

I gestured for her to move out of line with the door. She did so quickly. In spite of accord and agreements, Berliners were conditioned to react; it was a way of life. I got the door open in time to hear him polevaulting down the stairs. Her flat was a third-floor walkup, and he was out of sight. I saw there was no point in trying to catch him.

I closed the door and faced her. "Why didn't you tell me that first?"

She looked flustered. "I-I don't know. I guess I was more anxious to hear what you had learned, and I didn't know what to think of—of—"

"Of me?" I said.

She looked up at me with an expression that combined anticipation with a touch of fear and nodded.

"Well, professionally you need have no worries. As I said, there'll be no story until it's safe to tell it." I put my finger under her chin and raised it. "But otherwise, what is it you're worried about?"

You could say I'm always ready for most anything concerning love and war, but I wasn't ready for her reaction. She had her arms around my neck and her lips on mine with a kind of shuddering gasp. I'd stirred up something elemental in her that seemed to require urgent fulfilling. The parting of her lips said so, as did the pressure of her breasts and hips.

I'm not particular about the time of day or night when I lie down with a woman unless it interferes with business, and right now I couldn't afford to get entangled. I knew to simply put her off would do more than hurt her pride, it would put her off on me. I needed her confidence, but mostly I needed her Uncle Jan's address.

I picked her up, our lips still glued, and moved toward the daybed. I laid her down on its edge and knelt beside her, getting my lips free. "Listen," I whispered in English. "Our friend is back. I'll just be a minute."

I made it look real enough, charging out of the place, and when I stuck my head around the door again she was kneeling on the daybed, not knowing what to expect.

"I've got to see if I can follow him," I called to her. "Lock this door and be careful when you do go out. I'll give you a call."

And that was how Nick Carter sadly ran away from love with a delightful *fraulein* in the late afternoon.

CHAPTER 15

I gave Hilma ten minutes to simmer down before I called her. "Listen, honeychild," I said like a man in a hurry, "it might be a good idea if you stay close to home tonight. I didn't catch up with the spoilsport, but I'm going to have a talk with Wehner. Meantime, if you have any indication of problems, you call my hotel, okay?"

"Where will you be?"

"Hunting. One thing might be helpful—what's your uncle's address?"

There was a long pause. "What's that got to do with it?" The warmth was gone.

"Possibly everything. I don't have time to explain now. You'll just have to trust me."

She sighed. "I learned long ago not to trust anyone."

"You didn't learn very well. You've been trusting me so far."

"I had to."

"I think you still do. I'm sorry I couldn't stay. When I come back there'll be more time and no interruptions."

"Where are you going? Why can't you come back now?"

"I have to see the man who sent you to see me. That's why I need the address."

"You're not going to give it to him!"

"No, of course not. I'm just going to find out if he knows it already."

"If you get hold of a directory—"

"I've already done that. He's not listed. Remember, you said he'd moved."

"Do you remember the album of records on the player? Did you notice it?"

"One of my favorites."

"Number twenty-eight."

"Thanks. I'll be in touch soon." I hung up before she could respond. The album had been Puccini's *La Bohème*. Off of Clemett Gottwald Alle, all the streets in one section are named after composers. Uncle Jan lived at 28 Puccinistrasse—melodic as all hell.

Kraemer and nephew Horst had been killed because they had the photographs of the escapees. Hilma was in danger because they figured she'd recognize her uncle, and someone was going to take uncle's place. N12 had already spotted a plant amongst the photographs and had gone hunting. The plant was a hit man, and Uncle Jan's replacement was directing the operation. It wasn't really all that complicated, but before I went hunting myself, I thought I'd have a better look for the photographs, and then I'd pay Wehner a visit.

It had clouded over again, and the dusk light was the way I liked it, gray and diffused so bulk could be seen but detail obscured. The bulk of the police car was no longer in front of 18 Zimmerstrasse, and the lights on the other side of the Wall had yet to be turned on. My approach was a long one, first down Niederkirchner. Although Lutz's murder had not been front-page news in the morning papers, it had to be of obvious interest to BND, and I was damned if I wanted to rub gun butts with any of Wehner's boys, so I took it slow.

No effort had been made to repair the jimmied lock, and I went in like Flynn and took my good time going up the long flights. By the time I'd reached the flat, I knew I had the place to myself. The police and security boys had pulled out a lot of drawers and not bothered to push them back in. The large dried bloodstain on the rug was all that was left to mark the owner's passage, poor bastard. All he'd been trying to do was help.

I found nothing in the living room, bedroom or *salle de bain*. The windows facing the Wall had been crêped over, obviously by Horst, and the place was a kind of musty cave. I used a flash until I entered the storeroom. There the windows were free to let in the light, but even if it had been full daylight and I'd had all day, I couldn't have gone through everything there. There were three windows facing the street. The one on the Wall end had a cupolaed effect, curving outward with three separate panes. Through it you could see the guard tower on the East side and the reviewing stand on the West, a kind of coming-and-going window, I thought. I didn't like giving up the search, but I was willing to concede that Kraemer had had the photographs for safekeeping and they'd gone up in smoke.

I left the building by way of the hole in the wall in the cellar and had a close look at the tunnel. I went down into it and followed it for what seemed like an incredible distance. The earth was shored up with wooden planks, and in places it was starting to sift down. It wouldn't pass any safety tests, but it was one helluva job. If nothing else, they should all be getting engineering degrees out of it. I had the feeling that the only digging left to be done was straight up. I went back and sat on the dirt-hauling cart and smoked a cigarette. As long as the tunnel remained closed for a week, it didn't matter to me who came out of it.

Once the other side realized Allied intelligence was on

to their game, they'd have to call it off. They'd know that not only the plan, but it's purpose, has been compromised. If they tried to work it in some other way, the danger of exposure would not be worth it, not as long as the Kremlin was singing *détente*.

Whatever Wehner was up to, he was going to close down this operation tonight, and I was going to go find John Sparks. No AXE agent in the N rating would ever abandon a fellow agent if there was a chance of bringing him back alive, and there was that chance. Before I took it, I had a couple of stops to make.

CHAPTER 16

Lola's apartment lacked a concierge. It had the usual press-the-buzzer, speak-in-the-tube entrance.

"*Jah?*" Even strained through a tube her voice had that throaty come-get-me quality.

"Flowers for Fraulein Steinmetz."

"From whom, *bitte?*"

"One moment." I paused. "The card says, from Nicholas with love."

"Oh, bring them right up!"

The buzzer buzzed, the door clicked, and I went through into the foyer and the elevator.

She answered my ring, opening the door with a chuckle. "I knew it was you." She looked stunning in an elegant peignoir, her golden hair set in an upswing, the diamonds at her neck real.

"Well, come in, come in." She turned away. "Winty won't be here for another half hour. We're going to the ballet, the Stuttgart."

I closed the door as she turned toward me, arms wide.

"I think you've been awful not to answer my calls. What—"

I'd never thrown a bunch of yellow roses in a lovely woman's face, or even an ugly one's. In this case, it was a cruel waste of beauty. It was also a shock to Lola, as it was supposed to be. Her right arm rose late in instinctive reaction, her expression changing from sensuality to fear.

There was more to come. I backhanded her across the cheek so hard that as she cried out she spun around and fell against the chaise longue. I helped her complete the fall, coming down hard on top of her, one hand fastened in her beautifully styled hair, the other around the diamonds.

Her eyes bulged out, not only in fear, but also in the need for air. I had knocked the wind out of her, and I was giving her damn little chance to make up the loss. Her body and hands made futile upward thrusts against me. And then either she realized it was no use or she was half-strangled and could do no more.

"Lola, my love," I whispered, thrusting my hips down on hers, "why did you bug me in a moment of ecstasy? Who instructed you? Tell me." And again I punctuated the request with my hands. "If you don't, when Winty baby comes he can use those flowers at your bier."

I saw she was close to unconsciousness and released my hold on her throat. Her hands fell away from my wrists as she sobbed air into her lungs.

I gave her a moment before I tightened my grip. "Who, Lola?"

"Winty!" She gasped, as I knew she would.

"Why?" I supplied another punctuation mark and forced her legs apart with my knee.

"BND instructions!" Her voice was a pleading rasp.

I took my hands from her hair and neck and kissed her, forcing her lips open and blowing air into her lungs. She began to struggle again.

"You tell me all about it," I said. "That is, if you want to go to the ballet."

She was getting control of herself, getting angry. "There's nothing to tell! Get off me, you swine!"

"You tell me anyway, or when I get off, you won't be telling anybody anything ever. Understand?" I put my full weight on her, and she understood.

"Winty is BND section chief for Berlin."

"How do you know that?"

"He said so! He knew everyone I had known!"

"Had you met him when you were in BND?"

"No. Get off me, goddamm it!" She gave an upward thrust.

"Shut up!" I repaid her movement with my own. "Why did he tell you to do it?"

"He didn't give any reason. He said it was orders."

"But you're no longer BND."

"I-I owe him a lot. He set me up in business."

"Who were you setting me up for at the Osdorf?"

She shook her head, her hair looking better with the coiffure gone all to hell. "I don't know."

"Was that any way to treat an old friend?" I kissed her gently.

She began to cry, pushing at my chest, her legs widening a bit more under my weight.

My kisses began to gather momentum and intensity.

Her struggles reminded me of the girl who started out saying, "Please! . . . Don't! . . . Stop!" and ended up crying, "Please don't stop!"

Death and sexual passion are not unrelated. I had completely conquered her and nearly killed her and was now taking her by force. But very soon the force became mutual. She rose to me, spurred automatic magnetism between us. She could no more deny my intentions than she could prevent me from killing her. She hated me for what I had done to her, but now her shock sought healing, wanting me to give her sexual absolution. And when I entered her ruthlessly, her sobs were of need and not of fear.

It was a brief and violent encounter, as I wanted it to

be. I was merciless, and all too soon her choked cries of release faded, as did the frenzy of her body.

Exactly fifteen minutes after I'd entered the apartment, I offered her a cigarette. She took it, saying nothing, sitting on the chaise longue, trying to repair the damage to her appearance. What else would a woman do?

I gathered up the fallen roses and stuck them in a vase. "You expect your date at half-past?"

She tossed her head, hands at her hair.

"I think you'll do that better in the john. Your lipstick's a mess, your throat looks as if you've been strangled, and your diamonds are gone."

She made a startled search and found them between the cushions.

I stood in front of her. "Lola," I said, "you've been had."

She looked at me, eyes flashing angrily.

I laughed. "I should have said, past as well as present. Right now I'm talking about your benefactor. I'm surprised you didn't take the trouble to check his BND credentials. Maybe you didn't want to. A girl has to get along in this cruel, hard world. But your Winty is one of the bad guys, honeychild. And what you did nearly got me killed three times over."

Now she was paying attention.

"It's no way to treat an old flame. Did Winty say anything more about why he wanted me tenderly bugged?"

She shook her head. "No. Just that it was necessary. He said something about BND thinking you might be a double."

"He didn't mind your sleeping with me."

"No. He-he's a homosexual."

"That helps. I'm glad he was so generous with your favors. I just hope he hasn't had them. You scatter them around too much. You could be killing a lot of people with your kindness that way."

She stubbed out her cigarette. "What do you think I am, some goddamned whore?"

"Oh, you're much better than that, Lola, but I'm anxious to know if Winty has had you involved with any other Americans who could be doubles, say within the last week."

"No. This was the first time he'd ever asked me to do anything for him. He knew we'd met when I was in BND, so——"

"So all in the line of duty, even if duty was over, you agreed to play."

"Think what you like."

I smiled at her. "Like I said, a visit to the john is in order." I reached out my hand. "You'll stay in there repairing the damage until I let you out."

She ignored my hand, fear flaring in her eyes. "What are you going to do?"

"I want to talk to Winty in private. See how things are going with MFS."

She sucked in her breath, and I knew it wasn't in surprise, but at the thought of what I was going to do to him. I had to admit, it wasn't a nice thought.

Winty arrived with flowers too, an orchid that got mixed in with his teeth when I greeted his ring.

I was surprised at his size. He was taller and wider than I was. He had a close-cropped pelt of salt and pepper on top, a broad, florid face, and a beer-barrel body. I had the advantage of size; he, of bulk.

I had opened the door, shoved his hand holding the orchid into his grinning mouth, and hit him in the gut with everything I had. He was not only shaped like a beer barrel, but he was just as solid. Most men would have gone down on their knees and stayed there praying for air. He let out a grunt, spitting away the petals, his grin fixed.

My foot hitting his shin unfixed the grin, but not the determination in his heavy-lidded eyes. I had used the kick to block a groin kick on his part. He blocked my karate chop to where his neck might have been if he had had one, and I just avoided his counter aimed at taking off my head. Maybe Lola's concern had been for me.

"Well, Herr Carter," he said, going into a wrestler's crouch, "I told them to let me take care of you myself, and now here you are to let me do it, my dear." His voice was high pitched but not obviously gay. Still, it didn't go with his looks.

"I'd have come sooner, but things kept getting in the way." I feinted and hit him in the gut again. He winced and then laughed. I knew the only way to take him was to throw him off-guard, and that meant taking some punishment.

I let him hit me twice, and then I knew I couldn't afford the punishment. "We soften you up, *jah?*" He was enjoying himself.

I was sorry the ring wasn't larger, but Lola's living room was on the petite side. He feinted. I countered and launched a karate kick at his balls, knowing the effect would be just as painful, regardless of his sexual persuasion.

He took my feet on his thigh and rushed me. I dropped to the floor, rolled to the left, and tripped him. He stumbled and nearly fell. I came up behind him as he was getting his balance and gave him the kind of chop that breaks necks. He fell on his hands and knees for real, and when I booted him between the legs this time, he let out a shout of agony and crumpled, writhing on the floor, reaching for the offended parts.

I never take anything for granted. It helps me stay healthy. I didn't know how much of his torture act was phony. Further, time was important, and it was time to change tactics. When he stopped swearing in falsetto and sat up, I was sitting across the room with Wilhelmina in hand. "This will save wear and tear," I said.

He sniffed and rubbed the arm of his dinner jacket across his mouth.

"Listen carefully," I said. "You're going to answer my questions. If you don't, we're going to go into the kitchen and turn on the gas flame. I can toast you or shoot you, maybe both. It's up to you."

He looked at me, looked at the Luger, and shrugged. "What I know won't do you any good, because I know practically nothing."

"Who's your contact?"

"Colonel Jacob Hessmann."

"At Karlshorst?"

He gave me a dirty look. "Maybe Bonn."

"Don't get cute, Winty baby. What department?"

"Fourth," he muttered. Fourth was MFS's direct-action section. From AXE files I knew the name of the section chief. "Who's the head man?"

The sleeve across the mouth again, as if the taste of orchids were not so sweet. He looked ridiculous on the floor. "Colonel Helmut Pohl," he said.

"What were your orders?"

"To bug you. I want to get up."

"You want your balls shot off this time? Why did they want to bug me?"

He shook his head. "I don't know. They just called me in."

"How did you learn my name?"

"They knew it." His voice squeaked in scoffing. "They know everything. They even knew Lola knew you."

"Is she MFS?"

"No."

"What am I?"

He looked at me, smiling. "Aside from being an American pig, you are a military agent of DIA."

Inwardly, I sighed a bit. Despite all they knew, their agent in the NCS or the White House knew nothing about AXE, only my name.

"Get up, Winty. We're going to the kitchen and do a little frying."

Now there was a glint of fear. "No! I swear I'm telling you everything you ask."

"You're a lying sonofabitch." I stood. "Now get up."

He got on his knees, hands together as though in

prayer, and began to plead. "Herr Carter, I told you what you asked!"

I saw what was coming. As he catapulted himself at me, I jumped to the left. For all his bulk, he was very fast. He landed on hands and knees and dived for me again. I could have shot him, but there was more I wanted to know.

As he moved to come upright, I drop kicked. He went down thrashing, making painful sucking noises. Maybe he wouldn't be able to talk for a while, but he could still use his hands to write. Neither of the names he had given me were correct. We were going to start from the beginning, not just the bugging, but the killing, even if he was the next to die.

When I left Lola's apartment I had all the information he had to give. You could say I flushed it out of him. I had the feeling the Stuttgart ballet would be going on without either of them.

CHAPTER 17

The radio tower in West Berlin is a kind of Eiffel Tower filled with a great deal more than broadcasting equipment. High up on the tower, Paul Wehner has his SPD press office. Even on an overcast night it offers a panoramic sweep of the city, East and West.

I stood looking toward the East, my back to him, waiting for him to simmer down. Finally, he began to speak. "I was Lutz's case officer when he defected five years ago. After that, we saw each other from time to time. He wanted to join BND, but Bonn said no. He could be a double. In their mind, everyone is a double." His sarcasm was laced with schnapps. "Anyway, when he came to me and told me the plan, my immediate reaction was to stop it."

"Pity you didn't."

"Look, Nick, save your criticism. I don't need it. I'm telling you, that's all."

I didn't respond. I looked at the lights, geometric patterns, moving east.

"I discussed it with another friend. And for the reasons I have already told you, we decided to turn our heads the other way. I know the names of those who are escaping."

"You have their photographs."

"No. I know where the escape starts and where it ends. When you gave me the address, I tried to reach Horst. When I couldn't, I contacted Fraulein Raeder."

"You never saw the photographs." I turned from the window, concealing my disbelief by lighting a cigarette.

"I said we had to avoid being involved." He sucked on his pipe, his eyes avoiding mine.

I didn't say that having become involved, it would have been normal procedure for him to know everything, because obviously there wasn't anything normal about this. "When the escape took place, what were you going to do?"

"If it was successful, Lutz was to send word, and I would contact the police, who in turn would contact the press. The police would take the escapees into protective custody. The press would take statements, TV cameras, all the rest. After that we would come into it in normal fashion and start checking to see who was what. Now I suppose it will be Fraulein Raeder who will signal me."

"You know perfectly well that tunnel's compromised, Paul."

He stared at me. "Maybe, maybe not. Whatever happens, we can't lose on it."

"The escape was scheduled for the seventeenth, right?"

"It still is, and it will be best if you stay out of it. It has nothing to do with you, Nick. Out of past friendship and obligations I have—"

"It's been put off for a week."

"How do you know that? Why?" He set down his pipe, and I watched his hands closely.

"You'll be hearing the official why in the morning. Out of past friendship and obligations I'm telling you now. The President of the United States is going from the

NATO meeting in Brussels to Bonn; then he's coming here on the eighteenth for a surprise visit."

"What? *Gott in Himmel,* why?" He came up out of his chair, dumbfounded.

"The Youth Forum, *détente,* a gesture of goodwill. He'll go to the reviewing stand at Checkpoint Charlie, and supposedly Honecker will be on the other side. They'll wave at each other and make speeches."

"Jesus Christ!" He was praying, not swearing.

"Amen."

His face had grown flushed as the information sank home. "You see how it is!" he growled, snatching his pipe off the desk and marching to the window. "What bloody nonsense!" He swung around, the pipe between his teeth. "And you see, Bonn didn't even bother to inform me. Security is going to be an enormous problem."

"Just for that reason, Bonn hasn't been informed yet. The plan is to zip in and zip out."

"I hope you will forgive me, but it's goddamned idiocy!" His eyes were wide with anger and frustration. "Rather than stop the tunnel, I would stop the visit!"

"I haven't got time to argue policy. My job is to see that nothing nasty happens to my Commander-in-Chief."

"Well, you people take a helluva way to see to that!" he snapped. "This is our city! You give us no time to prepare."

"There are two schools of thought on it. Let the people know where number one is going beforehand, and you've got trouble, in a place like this. Let him pop in with normal security, and chances are good he'll survive."

"And in London and Paris and Bonn, he . . . ?"

"Look, Paul, I didn't come to debate. At least I've given you a head start. Just don't mention who's coming until you get the official word."

"I suppose it's called Allied cooperation." He slammed the pipe into the ashtray.

"I came to see you for two reasons—to see if you might have the photographs and records of the escapees and to tell you that von Winter works for MFS. You can pick him up at Lola's apartment. He's not in very good shape."

"We have nothing on him."

"I do, so do yourself a favor. He works for Reinke, chief of the fourth department."

"Jah. And what's he been doing for Colonel Reinke?"

"Trying to kill me, for one thing."

"Hah! What else?"

I laughed, not because there was anything funny about how upset he was, but because his anger was genuine, which proved to me that his sin was not double-crossing his own service, but growing too old in it. It made me feel better about him. "Ask me that tomorrow," I said. "And in the meantime, you'd better put some protective surveillance on Hilma Raeder."

As soon as I reached the street level, I called the Osdorf. Hilma had been trying to reach me. She'd phoned no fewer than six times. I left word to inform her, if she called again, that I was on my way.

I hailed a cab feeling a chill in my neck, which had nothing to do with the breeze.

CHAPTER 18

No one tailed us. I got off in a neighborhood of small shops and discotheques catering to undergraduates. With the youth forum in full blast the streets were filled with stoned celebrants, shouting their slogans of peace and brotherhood, figuring that the louder they shouted, the more meaning there was to what they had to say.

Threading my way through the crowd, I turned off and came to the narrow street that backed onto Hilma's flat. All the buildings in the block were the same. Each had its back patio with a high wooden fence and gate. The street was too narrow for more than one car. There was only one—the black Maria. It was blocking the opposite end of the alley.

I didn't bother with the gate. I took a short sprint and vaulted. I came down almost on top of the gate watcher. His reaction to my sudden appearance made him freeze momentarily—long enough for me to freeze him permanently. My arm went around his throat, and Hugo

111

went under his ribs to the hilt. I held him tight while he jerked and kicked away the last of his time. I quickly settled him into the flowerbed. He had a .45 with a silencer, which I placed on his chest in memorium. Then I moved on a run. I could only hope that she had followed my instructions and not opened her door to anyone.

I went from the back door down the main corridor to the stairwell and then up three flights, goaded by a grim fear. As I reached the top landing, I heard the killing cough of an automatic fired with a silencer.

There were three of them. The one farthest into the room had done the shooting. The other two were watching. I caught a glimpse of Hilma on the floor. As they swung toward me, I fired. The killer spun around, gibbering, his hands trying to plug the new hole in his head as he hit the floor. The one on my left got his hand on his shoulder holster and died as though pledging allegiance.

The third one got off one shot that hissed past my head. Then he went down, clutching his belly, bowing his head in final prayer for all his sins.

Hilma was lying half in the tiny hall that led to the bathroom. I saw that she had been hit high up above her left breast and was losing a lot of blood. I lifted her onto the daybed.

She opened her eyes. She was in shock, but she recognized me. "Nick," she wheezed and choked.

"Save the conversation, honey. You're going to be all right." I was glad to see there was no blood on her lips.

She shook her head. "Listen! Message came. . . . Escape can't delay. . . . Got to get out as planned . . . or get caught. Dieter and Jan know—" She faded away.

I had ripped off a piece of the sheet and torn away her bloody shirt as she whispered. I went to work, trying to slow the flow of blood. The bullet had penetrated just below the collarbone. I thought she'd make it.

Gunfire in a confined space makes a helluva racket.

Now that it had died away, people were coming to investigate. I could hear their cautious approach, their excited fluttering as they came up the stairs.

"Get an ambulance!" I shouted. "Call the police!"

That stopped them long enough for me to kiss Hilma goodbye and go on down the corridor to the bath. I knew there would be a window. I just didn't know what I'd find when I opened it. Not much. Three stories down and one roof up. I decided up was the shortest and quickest way. There was damn little on the concrete slab of the building to get toes and fingers into until I reached a projecting ledge. When I did reach it, I felt I was ready for Everest. Right above it was the roof's overhang.

I heard the siren as I levered a leg onto the overhang. The fire escape was on the far side of the building. By the time I dropped on its top and zipped down to the alley separating the building from the structure next door, a noisy crowd was gathered outside the front of Hilma's address. I joined the throng for a moment, long enough to see Hilma brought out on a stretcher and put in the ambulance, where they began giving her oxygen and blood. I noted the name of the hospital. The police were starting to swarm to break up the crowd, and I broke up with it.

Shouts of "Fascist pigs!" rose among the enlightened as I drifted away to a telephone kiosk. A recorded voice answered Wehner's phone. The office was closed for the day. If I wanted to leave a message I could speak at the tone. I had the feeling he'd done it on purpose, knowing I might call.

I spoke at the tone: "This is an urgent priority one. Our college team is at work again. Stop them. Nick."

I made one final call, this one to the CIA safe house. I gave identification to the voice on the other end and said, "With regard to our previous discussion, you have the equipment?"

"Yes."

"Have a driver bring it and pick me up in fifteen minutes at the corner of Sudatengente and Ansbacher, northwest side. Can do?"

"We'll be there."

CHAPTER 19

There is a point below the old Oberbaumberger Bridge, which spans the Spree, where pedestrians gather during the day to feed the swans. Surprisingly, the swans stay close to the western bank, night and day, and never cross the midpoint of the canal. The eastern side is a wall of faceless gray buildings, the glass gone from the windows, bars in some. The usual electric fence fronts them. The Spree is a major barge canal into East Berlin. When the barges and other shipping moves up and down the waterway, they are under close surveillance by DDR patrol boats.

The patrol boats are manned by a helmsman and two heavily armed lookouts, forward and aft. Anything they spot in the canal that is not readily identifiable, particularly if it is human, they shoot at—or they use special concussion grenades.

The patrol boats follow the barges to make sure no one jumps ship before reaching the control point. They are gray, low-slung boats. At night, running without lights and with throttled down diesels, they blend with the water and can be on top of you before you're aware of them.

I had requested from CIA an aqualung to go with a wet suit, flippers, and flash. But when I got in the Volks van that picked me up as arranged, there was no lung, only a snorkel.

"How come?"

The driver shrugged. "I don't know. I brought what was given me. I just obey orders. You want to take it back?"

I wanted to stuff it down his throat. "You know where to go?"

"*Jah,* the bridge."

"Well, drive around so I can see if this thing is big enough to get into." I had asked that the wet suit be large enough to fit over my suit. I found it a helluva tight fit. Shoes would go into leg pockets, Wilhelmina into a chest pouch. Goggles fit well, and the underwater flash was the latest ARV. Under four feet of water it could not be detected on the surface.

Schlesisch was the main thoroughfare paralleling the Spree, but a short block off it, running beside the canal, was Grobanstrasse. It ran under the span of the bridge and swung back onto Schlesisch, which was too well lit to suit me.

"You take your next left, get on to Groban, and I'll kiss you goodbye under the bridge," I said, watching the navigation lights of a barge going in the opposite direction.

"There'll be a patrol boat right behind him," the driver said, slowing down.

"Don't come to a complete stop, and when I get off, move away at the same speed."

"Somebody will have an eye on us. I'll slow to ten. Can you handle that?" He was enjoying himself.

There were no lights under the bridge. The barge had passed us, and I could see the bow light of another approaching. I opened the door.

"Good luck," he said as I went out, running crouched low, fighting the sudden shock and tripping effect of the pavement.

As soon as I had my equilibrium, I moved up under the metal span where the darkness was heavier. The white finger of a patrol boat's searchlight caught the rear of the van as it made its turn on the other side of the bridge, heading back on to Schlesisch. The light swung to the bank and swept it; then it moved higher. I lay flat, arms covering my face. I could practically feel its beam fingering me. After it had gone out, I rolled over on my back and waited.

I counted three ships passing, two going out, one going in, before they tried with the light again. This time they swept the canal first, but when they finally turned off this time, I knew they were satisfied that the van had not been doing something it shouldn't. With my eyes adjusted to the dark, I knew there were two boats patrolling the bridge quadrant.

They followed the traffic coming and going, and when there was no traffic they moved slowly in tandem, one along the east bank and one down the center. They were making certain no one left their Democratic People's Republic by the water route and arrived in the West alive. As for traffic going the other way, if anyone was that crazy, they had an eye out for that, too.

I had thought they were through playing with their searchlight, but suddenly it shot out, catching the swans in its glow where they congregated at the dock area. The swans cackled angrily and tried to move away. Their effort brought guttural laughter. Someone barked an order, and the light was doused. Sound carried clearly on the Spree. And with it I made my move.

I waited until the mutter of the diesels had started to fade; then I went barefoot down the incline, across the strip of road to the walled water's edge. In the water, I pulled on flippers, adjusted the mouthpiece, and submerged. I swam a short distance and surfaced. There was a strong current, right to left. The water was black velvet. I would have no vision without a light, and with the snorkel I couldn't get down to a no-show depth. I flung the snorkel back on the bank, took a deep breath, and went down. There would be no problem until I reached midpoint in the canal. Then it was going to be a matter of avoiding not only patrol boats, but also barge propellers.

The ARV, which I wore like a miner's light, cut the black, turning it to gray. I could see fish darting away from my approach. Hearing was my most important sense.

I surfaced for air and checked my course. My target was beneath the eastern span of the bridge. The current was even stronger than I'd first judged, moving me down from where I wanted to go. When I surfaced again, I'd be on the edge of the danger zone.

I went down, swimming hard at an angle. I could hear the approaching churn of propellers. Their heavy beat meant a barge. I surfaced to get a quick look and saw that it would pass me with enough clearance. I took in air and went deep, swimming on a parallel course so the current would not sweep me downstream while I waited for the ship and its sucker fish to pass. The heavy *thrum-thrum-thrum* of the barge's screws beat against my ears. When they began to fade, I listened for the softer beat of the patrol boat. I picked it up just when my lungs told me it was air time.

I switched off the ARV and rose, my back to the current so I could suck in air and get under fast. I saw that the light above was too light. It was the patrol boat's beam, trolling. I knew from the design of the boat that it carried radar but no sonar. The Spree was not built for submarine passage.

I could hear Hawk's dry rasp, "Well, when you go across, you won't have to worry about being depth charged."

Maybe, but right now I was worrying about getting enough air in my lungs to stay alive. I had stopped my forward motion to let the current drift me free of the probe. It seemed to be tracking me. My lungs were full of burning cotton. My throat constricted, and my ears were ringing. I couldn't stay down any longer. I forced myself to rise slowly, back to the light, which meant the beam might catch the top of my head but not my gaping mouth. I surfaced, saw torn cloud, drank air, and with flippers and hands, sank. I watched the dim stain of the searchlight move off, and I swam away on a tangent to the engine's sound. Before crossing midchannel I came up again for a look. I was in luck. Nothing was coming either way. I could hear a patrol boat moving up stream. I stayed on the surface and made time, using a modified breast stroke, aiming toward the silhouette of the bridge.

Aside from Hawk and those in the N section of AXE who had need to get into East Berlin the hard way, no one in the world knew where I was headed. That went for the KGB, GRU, MFS, and even CIA and BND. It was strictly an AXE secret. It had been learned from a German civil engineer, Carl Armfeldt, who had used it to escape from the Russians. Before the Second World War, he had been in the city administration. One of his jobs had been maintaining and building storm and sewer drains, some of which emptied into the Spree. So he knew an entrance to a drain that emptied into the Spree beneath the Oberbaumberger. No one else knew of it because the conduit had been completed during the war, and the maps on which it had been shown had been destroyed in the city's capture. One entrance to the drain was in a rubble-filled alley.

I had never used the route into East Berlin. And when the light hit me, I wasn't sure I was going to get the chance. The light didn't come from a patrol boat, but from a shore post. As I went under I figured I'd been picked up on some kind of surface scanner. Going deep, swimming with everything I could give it, I caught the sudden acceleration of a patrol boat closing in fast.

There would be no more surfacing. I had to reach the

drain exit now or not at all. My aim was to make contact with the edge of the canal first. The light on my head lit up grayness. The patrol boat thrashed by almost directly above me. I was beginning to hurt for air. The head beam offered nothing. I ignored what was going on above and concentrated on making contact.

As it was, I came within a stroke of plowing into the canal wall. I knew the drain emptied at the four-meter level, but I could only judge my depth by the pressure. I fought the current, fought the howling need for air as I swam parallel to the wall, my head toward it.

The ARV caught a change in coloration, a deeper hue. I swung inward. My hand caught the drain's top rim. I thrust down and forward, hands reaching. There was room for my body even though my knees banged on the conduit's bottom.

I went in, feet under me, feeling the upward slope of the drain. *Balls to the wall!* I thought. *What an epitaph—"Drowned in a sewer!"* Then my head came out of the water, and I opened my mouth to suck in air. What I sucked in wasn't air, but gas. I could hear the sounds I was making as I stumbled clumsily through the waist-high fluid, bent over by the low roof of the drain. I had to breathe, but all I was getting was poison rot. In the light of the ARV, the stinking tunnel began to bend and weave. Where the hell was the exit? The bloody German had said it was close to the canal. AXE had estimated no more than thirty meters.

I stumbled and fell and stayed down long enough to pull off my flippers. When I got up I began bouncing off the walls. My vision was going, and so was I. My lungs were all coughed up. If the light hadn't picked up the ladder indented in the drain side, I might have gone down to stay.

From some last reserve of strength I reached it and got my hands on its rungs. In a remote region of my mind, Nick Carter was commenting, *You know, of all the spots you've been in, of all the hard ones you've come up against, there's never been one closer than this.*

"Closer!" I muttered. "I'm still not out of it!" And I wasn't. Somehow I got up the ladder, thinking it was a conning tower in a submarine in which I'd been submerged too long. My hands fastened on the lid. I pushed up on it. And nothing gave.

Rage hit me. I'd asked for an aqua lung, and the best that everlovin' CIA could come up with was a useless snorkel! I put my back into the lid. I put everything Nick Carter had left into it. Every muscle in me shouted, "Open up, you bastard!"

The lid moved, and I forced it up an inch. Through that inch came cool night air. Fresh air! I drank it in like a dried out wino with a keg of redeye. After the dizziness and gagging settled down, I went at it again, and the lid rose, to show me a circle of sky with a single star in it.

CHAPTER 20

I lay amid the rubble between two blank building walls, letting my strength come back, feeling it flood in on a tide of night air. It had been a very near thing. After a few minutes, I sat up and unzipped the wet suit. It stank. I got Wilhelmina and my shoes out of the thing and hung it on the top rung of the ladder with the ARV. I lowered the lid and piled over the rubble covering that had nearly made the place my coffin.

I didn't think N12 had used this route to East Berlin—no wet suit, no indication. If he'd been drowned, some word of it would have leaked. Enough of speculation. I finished tying my shoes and stood up.

I was in a high-security area. The buildings that flanked me ended at the Spree, and the alley was blocked by a high wall. The buildings were MFS property, manned day and night by Vopo Spree-watchers. The alley came out onto Stralauer Allee, whose overhead Straben-bahn I was counting on to give me some much-needed cover. I only had a short way to go on it. The building on my right bordered Warschauerstrasse, part of an arterial ring that, before the Wall, had circled the inner city. Now no transportation crossed the bridge but the U-Bahn, and no West Berliners were permitted to make the crossing without the proper documents.

My goal was the U-Bahn station at Warschauer Platz. It was about a kilo, or little more than a half mile, from where I was. It didn't sound like much to get there, except for two things. The area was well lit and under constant patrol.

Stralauer had a new row of apartment buildings facing the security block. The buildings had an ersatz quality. They housed Vopos and their families. The elevated track running above the center of the street helped to tone down the street lights.

I crossed to the apartment side as a train clattered by overhead. I started moving toward the main artery. I was halfway there, when a two-man patrol turned the corner. Before they could get close enough to have a good look at me, I tossed them a wave of greeting and turned in toward the apartment house on my left. It was a four-story affair full of ice-cube windows and varied hues. I was in luck—the front door was not completely closed, possibly bad workmanship on purpose.

I went into the narrow entrance hall, leaving the sound of jackboots on pavement and a voice calling, "You there, halt!" I followed the corridor to the back of the building. The confined smell of boiled cabbage and sauerkraut made me glad I wasn't planning to stay. The back door let out into a paved play area blocked by the rear of another building stamped out of the same mold. Its rear door was locked.

I had no time to be subtle. Wilhelmina's butt got rid of the pane nearest the knob. The falling glass hitting the floor made as much noise as Big Ben on a foggy night. It was my night for patrols. I went through the building and out the front into the arms of a three-man team having a cigarette.

"Something is not right," I announced before they could exhale. "A window in the rear door has been smashed. Someone may have broken in. Could you come, *bitte?*"

Cigarettes went sailing, and the three charged past me, eager types. They would probably meet up with the pair on my trail. Words would be exchanged, and the hue and cry would hit the fan.

There was no one on the street, so I legged it to Warschauer. Then I had a long block to go to reach the U-Bahn station.

At that hour it wasn't all that bad. There was some traffic, shops were open, and I wasn't alone as I crossed to the far side. I walked quickly. To jog or to run would immediately attract attention.

As I entered the station, I heard a siren start to wail. I also heard a train rumbling in below and joined others going down the steps two at a time. It was obvious that when the siren sounded, everyone was anxious to make themselves scarce. I got off at the first stop, as did a good many others, and switched to the S-Bahn, staying on it until it pulled in at the junction on Frankfurter Allee. There I changed again to the U-Bahn and stayed on board until it came into the Alexander Platz. From there I planned to walk to 69 Schützen. It would be nice to find N12 tending bar there.

To reach the café I had to leave the crowded thoroughfare of Leipziger and walk three blocks down Freidrichstrasse toward the control point as though I was planning to go through the Wall into the West zone.

I had timed my approach to coincide with the usual theatergoers who had come into East Berlin for the evening to see Brecht or whoever and then departed around 2330, before the midnight shutdown of the exit point. Most of them drove, but a few were pedestrians like myself, so it was no sweat. I turned the corner into Schützen, and there was number 69, the Café Gottwald. It had been built as a projection on the government building that filled most of the block.

There was a small marquee that looked like the entrance to a public latrine. The door was white in the glare of a single bulb. The outdoor facilities had been tucked away for the night, but inside I could hear shouts and laughter. Someone was having a good time in the old town tonight.

I opened the door and went in. The interior lighting was practically nonexistent. Cigarette and cigar smoke layered the air. To my left was a bar with three stools, none occupied. Along the wall to the right was a line of wooden tables but most of the tables were clustered beyond, cluttering back into the gloom. All of them appeared to be filled with off-duty Vopos in various stages of getting drunk. I saw no female customers.

The raucous pitch of sound had dwindled as I'd entered. Now, as I moved toward the bar, it picked up again.

The bartender wore a white apron. Over his blue shirt he wore a leather vest. He was razor thin, a pointed man with pointed ears, eyes, nose, chin. His mouth was a slit in his axlike face, and with his cropped hair arrowing to a V, he had the look of a starved wolf. I wouldn't have been surprised if he'd howled in response to my order for a stein of pilsner blond. The sweating waitress who came to the bar and banged down a half dozen empties gave me a cold, speculative glance as she bawled for a refill. She had plenty of bulk. Her arms hefty, and her small pouched eyes blinked redly against the smoke and sweat. "*Schwein!*" I heard her mutter.

Her partner said nothing, filling the glasses from the tap. I took them for husband and wife. When she was gone, and I'd had a sip, I said, matter-of-factly, "I'm looking for an old friend."

He was busy sudsing out steins.

"I'd hoped to meet him here last Wednesday, but I got delayed in Jena."

The pointed man kept his pointed head on his work.

I glanced toward the huddle of customers. "He wasn't military. He was a tunnel engineer."

He still didn't look up, but I saw the momentary reaction.

"We agreed if I couldn't make it on Wednesday, we'd make it tonight."

He had finished with the steins and now set them on the drain section of the counter. He wiped his hands on his apron and reached for his cigarettes, giving me a pointed-eyed glance.

"No one has been here asking for you," he said. His lips didn't move.

"I haven't told you my name."

"It doesn't matter. No one has come here asking for anyone."

"My friend is tall but not so thin as you. He has a streak of white in his hair, like so." I indicated.

The pointed man shook his head. "I have seen no one like that. You have the wrong place."

"He might have left a message for gold tip." I flipped open my case, tapping one of my special gold tips on it.

I lit up and turned in my chair, taking in the scene as the waitress came out of the smoke hefting her tray of empties. Obviously the pair had to be in on the escape, and I couldn't blame the pointed man for wanting none of me. I couldn't help but get a kick out of the wonderful enormity of making the café the escape point, even if the opposition knew all about it.

I sipped my beer slowly, wanting to give him time to think me over. The really dangerous part of it was that since the MFS was in on the plan, these two were undoubtedly under watch, and anyone approaching them would be under watch too.

When his bride stamped away with another load of

suds, I turned to face him again. He was back working on the empties.

"Well," I said, "do you have a message for me?"

He gave a slight shake of his head. There was new sweat on his brow.

I finished my beer. "I'll have another," I said.

He was not anxious to give me one. He was sure I was MFS, and I couldn't blame him.

"Well, I have a message for you," I said. "The eighteenth is going to be a very bad day unless your memory improves fast."

His hand shook as he stubbed out his cigarette. He was in a helluva fix. His pointed eyes seemed to glimmer.

"Hey, you!" A loud voice snapped from in amongst the Vopo throng.

The pointed man's arms jerked, slopping water from the sink onto his apron. His head swiveled toward the command.

"Easy does it," I sighed.

"I mean you at the bar!" A chair went over with a clatter as the sound in the room died away raggedly. I heard jackboots parading down the room.

"You!" the voice proclaimed. "I'm talking to you!"

He was a sergeant, red-faced, pig-eyed, half-drunk, and mean. His uniform was open at the neck. I could smell the stink of him.

"Well, you shouldn't be so loud about it," I said, rising. "I heard you the first time. What do you want?"

He blinked. His face got redder. The raw gash of a mouth twisted angrily. "Who the hell do you think you are? This happens to be a private club!"

"I did not see the word *private* on the door. I was not aware there were private clubs in the German Democratic People's Republic." I stood looking down at him coldly.

He couldn't quite get a handle on it, but the silence made him realize he'd better do something or lose a lot of face. "Who the hell are you, anyway?"

"I'm Ernst Platz, senior-grade state engineer," I snapped.

"Senior Engineer Platz, hey! And what do you do, Senior Engineer Platz?" he sneered.

"I dig tunnels for the Ministry of Power. Now go away." I turned from him and sat down.

Someone coughed, and someone snickered. Those were the only sounds for a moment. Then the sergeant, his voice hissing with rage in my ear, commanded, "Your identification, *mein Herr* Engineer!"

"Go away," I said, lifting my stein with my left hand.

As I knew he would, he grabbed my arm and tried to spin me around. As I came around and up, the beer went into his face and a short right wiped it off. He went spinning down the room and hit the floor in front of his comrades.

Out of the corner of my eye, I saw that the pointed man had turned to stone, his head bowed as though in prayer.

Before anyone could move I stamped my foot, clicked my heels, and shouted, "Achtung!" Then I strode toward them and the fallen warrior, who was having trouble getting up.

"Now, all of you listen to me!" My manner had to be convincing but not overdone. "I realize you are off-duty and relaxing. Good. I have no reason to interfere. But this fool is drunk, and he sets no example for anyone. I could have him sent to a correction camp if I chose. I am not only Senior Engineer Paltz; I am also a colonel in the Third Oberkommando Reserves. Now, let's have no more of this, unless someone is looking for serious trouble."

I didn't look down at the sergeant, who was an unsteady phoenix, rising. I turned on my heel, knowing the bluff wouldn't hold. It sounded like something out of an old late-show movie—"I'm the son of the greatest swordsman in all France!" Sooner than later someone was going to be demanding proof of my rank, and it wouldn't be a drunken sergeant.

"My bill," I said to the pointed man. He didn't look up. "You dig tunnels?"

"On special occasions."

"What direction do you dig them?"

"I like to go from west to east."

"You'd better get out of here," he sighed.

"Right now I'm looking for my friend." I plunked some coins down on the bar.

"You have no friends here." He swept up the coins.

"Did he leave a message?"

I heard a chair shoved aside, heard the sound of approach, saw there were two of them this time. I was ready to reach across the bar and grab pointy by his Adam's apple, on which I would undoubtedly cut my hand. He moved away as the two Vopos sat down on either side of me.

"Guten nacht," I said to the pointed man, and jerked my head at the reinforcements, both corporals, both reasonably sober, sharp-looking.

"One moment, if you please Herr Colonel," the larger of the two said, with the accent on *colonel*. He remained seated.

"Yes, what is it, Corporal?"

"I do not wish to be rude, Colonel, but may I see your identification?"

"For what reason?"

The corporal shrugged. "Orders. Everyone this close to the Wall must be prepared to show his identification."

Yes, I thought, particularly any civilian strangers who pay late-night visits to the Café Gottwald.

"Who is your commanding officer?" I said.

"Captain Tobler." It was so quiet in the room that you could hear the cigarette smoke rising.

"Suppose you take me to him."

"I can't do that. My orders are to stay here."

"Very well," I said, and reached in my pocket.

There was a single overhead light in the center of the ceiling, one of those old-fashioned half-moon jobs. I swung, shot it out, backhanded the butt of the Luger down on the corporal's head, and threw a punch with it at his pal. In the blackness I felt some teeth give as he went down, taking the chair with him.

The bedlam was instantaneous and unfriendly. There would be a stampede in my direction. I vaulted the bar and landed beside its crouching attendant. "Which way out!" I whispered urgently.

"Down!" He pulled me lower as I felt him fumbling. Then a floor trap came up, framing a square of gray light.

I gripped his pipestem arm in thanks and dropped through, figuring this was where the tunnel was to come up.

He stuck his head down after me. "Your friend said 28 Puccini."

With the trap shut, I went down on all fours and scuttled toward a lighter area in the rear. By the time I reached it, I could hear a whistle blowing shrilly at the front of the place. The café had a cinderblock base, and there was a narrow opening with the trap gone.

The point of exit was not exactly choice. It was an open infield area facing the Wall. The only shot I had was to use the massive building adjoining the café as a shield and hope that no one came around its far end before I reached it. I made it all right and used the building next to it in the same manner.

By the time I'd managed to cross Shützen and start angling back toward Leipziger, sirens were in full cry. Fortunately, the pursuit had never got untangled from its beer steins.

CHAPTER 21

Lutz was dead and Hilma badly wounded because the real Jan Steuben was unable to stand up. Whether he was tucked away in a cell at Karlshorst and had been replaced by a double or was being permitted to carry on as usual, remained to be seen. It remained to be seen, because real or fake, he was the only connection I had left in trying to locate N12.

Steuben's address was in the Weibensee district, which meant another Bahn ride. It didn't bother me. It gave me time to think.

Hawk and I knew that N12's message had been tied in with an assassin, an assassination, or both. The café address he had left confirmed it. The attempt would come via the tunnel; the victim would be the President. It wasn't present evidence alone that led to that conclusion. I had read N12's file on JFK's death. It detailed N12's pursuit of a second assassin on the scene at Dealey Plaza that November noon in 1963.

N12 had worked on an angle other investigators had

pretty well ignored. Right after Oswald had returned to his rooming house and was upstairs, a police car had stopped out front. It had tooted its horn, paused, and then had driven away. When Oswald left the house a few moments later, he first stood on the curb as though waiting for someone. When no one came, he walked away. Some blocks later he met a second police car. This one was driven by Officer Tippit, whom Oswald first approached as though he knew him. A few seconds later he gunned Tippit down.

N12 had learned that the Dallas Police had sold two of their patrol cars in April 1963. One of them bore the number 170—the number Oswald's landlady had said was on the patrol car that had stopped outside her house. N12 went looking for the car. He traced it to Mexico City. He traced it to two Castro DGI agents, a Mexican and an American with a German background. Before he could call for support, he got trapped in a shootout. He killed the Mexican and one of the Cubans before he went down. With four slugs in him, it was a long time before he was up again. By then the trail was as cold as a dog's nose in January.

Old John Sparks, N12, had found his German-American again. That's the way I figured it. The presidential hit man was out to double his score. The question was, had he found N12?

Jan Steuben's house backed on to a cemetery and was bordered on one side by a large children's park. Maybe there was a double meaning in it. His house was cut from the same mold as all the other houses on the short block—small, with a high peaked roof, a kind of tec-built *volkstraumen*. It had a patch of lawn with a tree and waist high shrubs as a border. It faced toward Gounodstrasse, but somehow I didn't think either composer would have been particularly flattered. There were dim streetlights at either end of the block.

The neighborhood showed that although everyone was

equal in the DDR, some were equal on a higher level; but even in being higher, everything must conform.

There was no car in front of the Steuben's, no light in any window, just as there was no light in any of the adjoining houses.

I turned in and went along the walk and followed the branch to the back. I moved as though I owned the place. The bordering shrubs at the rear gave the little yard some privacy from the vast marble orchard beyond. The crosses marched away mutely. They could offer helpful cover if the need arose.

I had two windows and a door to choose from. If one was bugged, they were all bugged. I chose the door. I had no key that would fit the lock, and I didn't want to waste time picking it. My pocket equipment included a small glass cutter and a roll of masking tape, a strip of which ensured that the glass would not fall inward.

It took a half a minute to do the job. The inside lock opened smoothly, and I was in the kitchen with the door closed behind me before you could say, *"Geschwindigkeit."*

There wasn't much downstairs. A hallway, a combination living room, whatever, a closet, and stairs. There would be two bedrooms and a john above. There was no place for anyone to hide out.

The stairs were not carpeted, and they creaked. I went up them homing on the hefty snoring. Their bedroom door was open, and Uncle Jan and his wife were sleeping in their featherbed. They might be in a jam, but that wasn't going to stop them from sleeping.

The door to the other bedroom was closed. I had a look there first, on the off chance that John Sparks was a houseguest, but I didn't expect him to be. The room was empty, and the whole place shrieked of normalcy. My seventh sense wouldn't buy it. But it was possible that Steuben wasn't aware he had been replaced—that he wouldn't know until he arrived at the café.

There was a low footstool near the door. I took it with

me to the head of the bed and sat down. By the halflight from the window, I could see that this Jan Steuben was the same Jan Steuben I had given the signal via the tour guide.

I woke him by shaking his arm gently. The snore snapped off. He gulped and came awake, his body going rigid. His startled eyes blinked at me in the dark. There was no sound or movement from his Frau, even when I began whispering to him.

"Herr Steuben, I come from friends on the other side. No need to fear."

He started to rise, and I eased him back.

"I'm from Hilma."

"Hilma!" he gasped, trying to come up again.

His wife stirred and rolled over. "Jan, what is it?" she cawed, still asleep.

"Nothing!" he whispered furiously. "Lie still!"

"I'm looking for a friend of mine." I described N12's furrow.

"Gott in Himmel!" He suddenly came out of it, grabbing my wrist. "Get out of here! This place is under watch! There are devices!"

"Easy!" I ordered. "Just tell me, did my friend come?"

"Jan!" his wife sat up, staring at me.

"Shut up, woman! Lie down! Yes, your friend came. They caught him, just the way they'll catch you! Why are you here!"

"Was he alive when you saw him last?"

"I-I don't know. He fought them, and then they threw his body in a van. For the love of God, man, get out of here!" He was now holding my wrist with both his hands.

His wife was sitting up again, breathing hard, her eyes fixed on me.

I got up. "Don't worry about the tunnel."

"They know all about it. They have forced me to— to . . . !"

"I know, but the digging has been called off. There'll be no escape."

He sat up. "I don't understand. I was told tonight to be ready for the eighteenth. I'll be leading people into a trap!" It was true, tunnel or no tunnel.

"Don't worry. Sorry to have disturbed your sleep."

"Go! Go!" he cried out as I went, my last picture of them two white wraiths sitting up in bed.

My only hope was to get into the cemetery, but not horizontally. They would expect me to leave by the back, so I went out the front. I got as far as the shrubs before they rose up and hit me like a swarm of bees, coming in from all sides. I fired twice before I went down under a steel front. To struggle was futile, so I struggled anxious to leave an imprint. The imprint was on the other foot, fist, and club. It had to be the latter that exploded my skull and blew me into nowhere.

CHAPTER 22

The cell had nothing going for it. A four-by-eight with a wall-bracketed slab on which I was lying. The motif was solid gray cement. There was no barred window. Air came in through a ceiling duct. An overhead bulb supplied a pale blue light. There was a plastic bucket in the corner. No one had thought to turn up the thermostat, and with nothing but my shorts to keep me warm, the frost was on the pumpkin.

My return to the living was one of those things. I had been swimming up through a red sea of pain, which had become the Spree, its water turned to lava. With consciousness, my thought process took a delicate hold on reality. I lay still adjusting to the pain in my skull and the battered condition of my body. There was one consolation—someone wanted me alive. Also, one realization penetrated the unpleasantness. I was very hungry. Hunger signaled the passage of time. It disturbed me because of what Steuben had said. It meant the digging was continuing. He could be wrong, but I couldn't bank on it, because I couldn't bank on anything. Whatever the answer, I had to get out of this massage parlor.

It took some practice to stand. Then it took some far more difficult practice to start rubbing out the kinks. The boys had obviously used me as a football, and although nothing was broken, everything felt badly bent. It was the kind of situation in which AXE conditioning and years of training pays off.

While I worked myself back into operation, I concentrated on deep breathing. Pierre was my secret weapon. I knew I might have to use him in mixed company. So with the knee bends and pushups and leg drops, I breathed deep and began holding in. My swim across the Spree had loosened things up in that department.

The cell door had the usual grate for food to be shoved in and a peephole to assure that the captive was behaving. I could assume that I was under observation and that my activity was going to attract attention so the MFS goons could question me. If no one got interested in my physical-fitness program I was going to start a protest rally that I hoped would bring more than the order to shut up. But I figured the first would happen, and it did.

As I heard the door being unbolted, I moved quickly to the wall bucket. When the two chaperons entered, they found me with my back to them, relieving myself.

"Be right with you," I said.

It wasn't what they had expected, which was what I had expected. I turned to them, and they stood staring at me.

"Well, you could have knocked."

"Come on, get out!" The larger of the two gestured angrily, moving toward me, billy club in hand.

In the blue light my assorted bruises and welts bore a brownish tinge. Marching along the drafty corridor under normal lights, they took on a more colorful hue. My stomach muscles felt as though some bastard had used them to kick field goals. My head throbbed and ached within bearable limits. I had palmed Pierre at the bucket.

There was little point in putting him to use in the highways and byways of Karlshorst. I couldn't very well expect to get out of this noted KGB-MFS security complex dressed as I was. Further, a prison corridor was no place to start dropping gas bombs, particularly when I was obviously being taken to some other place than the gallows.

We went up three long flights, emerging from the bowels of the joint. I saw that it was still dark out but with maybe a faint hint of dawn. I was damned if I could figure out why being worked over so thoroughly had made me hungry. The fact was, I felt starved. My condition indicated I'd been out of the play for a long time.

I began to pant and slowed my pace, looking for reaction.

The big one growled, "Keep moving, you!"

" 'Fraid I'm not as strong as I used to be." I stumbled against him.

"Shut up!" He grabbed me by the arm, and I sagged, making the other one take hold to keep me up.

One thing was for sure—they were under orders not to damage the goods further.

We were on the ground-floor level, moving along a glassed-in connecting link. Outside lights lit up the landscape, giving it an exposed, naked look, as they were supposed to, so the comrades inside could feel safe from the comrades outside.

At the end of the hall were two guards before a double door. They might as well have been carved out of wax for all their reaction at our approach. Then, just as we arrived before them, one proved that he was alive by turning and giving a couple of solid whacks on the door.

We were expected. The muffled order came for us to enter. The unwaxed guard turned the knob and shoved. The door opened, and we went in.

It was a well-appointed office with wall-to-wall carpeting that felt good under my cold feet. There was a single exit in the far left corner. Like the corridor, it had windows on either side, but in this case the drapes had been pulled.

Two officers awaited our arrival—a colonel sitting behind a large ornate desk that dominated the room and a major sitting on a handsome leather couch, backed by the window on the right. On the desk were five objects—Wilhelmina, Hugo, tool kit, passport, and ID cards. There was also an electric clock-calendar. It hit me hard. It explained my hunger. The time was 0330. The date was the eighteenth. I'd lost an entire day!

The two officers said nothing, examining me. The two escorts had faded back but remained in the room. Outside I could hear rain pecking at the windows. Inside, I was damned if I was going to break the silence.

The colonel had a thin, wolfish look and glittering narrow eyes, the Heydrich type. I recognized him from an AXE filmstrip. He was Reinke, head of the fourth department. The major was about my size, stolid and humorless looking. I didn't know him.

Colonel Reinke decided his stare wasn't going to turn me to ice even if the air conditioning did. "Herr Carter," he said in high, lisping voice, "your passport and identification papers say you are a journalist. We know differently, of course. There is only one additional point we wish to clear up. How did you get into the Eastern zone last night?"

He'd confirmed his calendar. I'd explore it. "Last night?" I rubbed my head.

"Yes, yes. We thought you'd like a nice sleep." He had a mouth like a fly trap.

So I'd been drugged. "How? I don't understand."

"If you want to play games, Herr Carter, we can teach you a few. But in the interest of *détente* and relaxing tensions, we thought it would be easier like this. It's very late, and Major Nebe and I wish to retire. Now, how did you get here?"

"You won't believe it, but I swam."

"No, I don't believe it!" Thin patches of color showed on his flat cheeks.

"Okay, I came in on a tour through Checkpoint Charlie, and I just didn't go back."

"You came in a tour bus in the afternoon, and you left at 1520 hours. How did you return? I'm all through with being polite, Herr Carter."

"What kind of car do you drive?"

His answer was automatic. "A Mercedes 450SE. What's that got to do with it?"

"Someone driving the same kind of car came into West Berlin this after— I mean yesterday afternoon. One of your officers making an official call. I don't know who he was, but I came back in his trunk."

Reinke glanced at Nebe and then back at me. "What was the license number?"

"BL466."

"Check on it." He tossed the command at the major. Nebe went out the rear door.

"What were you doing at Herr Steuben's house?"

"Trying to find a colleague of mine. We're working on the same story."

He opened a desk drawer and flipped a Polish passport on it. He opened it so I could see N12's photo. "This colleague, hey?"

"No. Another American like myself."

What passed for a smile cracked his lips. "Oh, he was an American, I have no doubt. Did you really think you could stop the tunnel from being completed?"

I returned the smile. "Did you really think you could get away with injecting an assassin into the group? BND, DST, SIS, CIA, DIA," I recited. "We all know that your fourth department, Colonel, is a cover to control and inject terrorist squads and hit men into the West. We know your connection with the Baeder Meinhoff gang, with the PLO, with Carlos, and so forth and so forth."

He'd been looking down at his hands. Now he looked up. "I'm impressed," he said sarcastically. "The only types who will be on hand to greet refugees at the western end of the tunnel in a few hours will be the fools who dug it. The BND station chief, Wehner, suffered a serious accident. He was run over before he could halt the digging. We know." Again the smile. "His second is one of ours."

"Do you really want to start World War III with the assassination of our President?"

"I seem to recall that a previous assassination of your President started no wars. How can you start a war when the assassin is one of your own?"

"Not one of ours, but one of yours."

"And who can prove that?" He shrugged. "Not your friend, who is on his way to Lubyianka, and you, whom I think we'll take care of right here."

"Malarkey!" I scoffed. "You think only your side knows about this tunnel? BND knew about it from the time it started, and we've all known about it. Those people are going to run into a screening process that will get the man my government has been after since a November afternoon in 1963."

That caught his attention. He stubbed out one of my cigarettes, staring at me.

"And when we get him and he confesses—and he will, you know that—what's that going to do for the DDR, the Soviet Union, and *détente?* What's it going to do for you, Colonel? If you're smart, you'll call it off before the shit hits the fan."

For a couple of seconds my bluff had him uptight. Then he snorted down his long nose and said, "Pah! If that was the case, you wouldn't have come over here as you did, no more than that other stupid agent, and you wouldn't have tried to have Wehner stop the digging."

The door opened, and the major came in, looking pleased and excited. "He's lying. There is no such license number."

I let all the air out of my lungs and then quietly inhaled so that the overflow came up to my teeth.

"Oh, yes there is," I said. "Look." I extended Pierre.

Colonel Reinke leaned forward and collapsed on his desk, sliding down to the floor. The major stepped toward him and spun in. The surprised guards surged toward me and hit the floor with a mild clatter. I turned off Pierre's valve, put him on the desk, and got to it. I stripped off the major's pants and put them on. The fit was good enough. His identification went in the rear pocket. He was unbooted, wearing shoes and socks. They went on next. The closet supplied his trench coat. I buttoned it to the top. His garrison hat was slightly large, which was good—its brim would give my face better concealment. All my equipment on the desk, plus N12's passport, went into coat pockets. Now all I needed was the colonel's car keys and some fresh air. The keys were in his pants pocket. They didn't want to come out. My head was feeling like a yoyo. I was soon going to have to give in to the aching need to breathe.

I rose with the keys in hand, a portion of pocket material with them. My last gesture before I turned off the lights and departed the room by the rear entrance, was to recover my cigarette case from the floor where the colonel had dropped it.

The door closed behind me with a solid thunk, and I drank up most of the air in the corridor. It was very short, closed in, and it ended with double glass doors opening on to a marble foyer and a main exit.

There were two guards on the doors, and they snapped to as I went by, head lowered, busy lighting a cigarette. Back from the main exit was a podium with a signout roster, its guardian sitting in a glassed-in office cubicle. He saw me approaching and came forth. I hoped Pierre had enough left to offer one for the road. The podium guard snapped to, clicking his booted heels and throwing a salute. I threw it back at him.

He stood at ease and started flipping pages. "Identification please, Herr Major," he said.

I was grateful that the only real lighting came from his

office. I handed him Pierre. He held it up in surprise. As I plucked it away he went over flat on his face.

"Hey!" I shouted. "Help!"

The guards came off the door in a blitz, in time for the last play.

The outside lighting was a dull glare in the rain. The parking lot was off to my left. At this hour there was only one Mercedes 450SE to be seen. I went toward it, running, which looked natural enough in the downpour.

CHAPTER 23

Karlshorst had been the KGB center of East German control since the end of World War II. As such it is a maze of walled compounds, all of which deal security. I'd been a guest of the East German, MFS, fourth department, and was now driving the head man's car. Security on the exit gate would be tight. Aside from having the wrong looks, my trench coat indicated I was a major, not a colonel. It was going to be touchy, providing I got to the gate before the alarm went off.

The road, like everything else, was brightly illuminated. I checked Wilhelmina and tucked her barrel under my leg, the butt extending for an easy move. Anyone looking in the window would not see the Luger. My hand would be on the shift lever. I put Nebe's wallet with his official identification on the window ledge. The exit point loomed up, and I began easing to a stop. The guard house was, as I had expected, a cement block with twin steel gates of the railroad-crossing type, raised and lowered by a switch inside the post.

I came to a stop as a massive hulk of East German MP opened his sliding door and stepped out. Through the fogged glass, I could see he had a twin inside. As I lowered the window halfway, he leaned forward and flipped me a quick salute.

I returned it, holding out the open wallet with my left hand as I turned my head toward the dashboard radio, fiddling with the tuning knob.

For a moment I thought the next move was going to be mine. He stood there in the bucketing rain, studying the identification as though he'd never seen it before.

"Come on! Come on, Corporal!" I snapped. "I want to get some sleep."

The wallet came back in. I snatched it and tossed it on the seat. He straightened up, heels clicking over the hiss of the rain, and threw me another highball. Since he didn't have much else to do, he had it perfected.

I growled and cranked up the window, waiting for the gates to rise. The wait drew out. Nothing moved but my windshield wipers. There was a faint gray smudge in the east, and before those bastards moved it was going to be daylight. Something had gone off the track.

I cranked the window down to head level and shouted, "You in there! Raise those gates and right now!"

"Sir"—the corporal stuck his head out the door—"we are getting no answer from the main building. You know the orders, sir."

"I know the orders, and I'm giving you one right now! Raise those gates, or I'll have your head on a platter!"

The corporal hesitated. Orders are orders in any army, but rank has its privileges, particularly just before dawn.

"Now!" I roared.

The MP called over his shoulder, "Hans, raise them," and thereby buried his chances for promotion forever.

The access road from the gate reminded me of the CIA access at Langley up onto route 123—a straight shot of road, heavily illuminated and studded with trees. I had just reached its end and swung on to the highway, when school let out. A siren began to wail and then another.

I switched on the two-way radio and monitored the alert. It took 'them a couple of minutes of scrambling to figure out that I was in Reinke's car, clear of the compound. By that time I was rocketing down the Treskow autobahn. I knew if I could reach the Rennbahn—the racetrack—and get into the woodlands of the Ober Schöneweide before they threw a chopper up to spot me, the odds might be acceptable.

But I was driving one of only a very few cars on the road, and the only one that seemed intent upon becoming airborne. I heard the orders go out to get six slingwings up. They had the area down cold. Patrol units were being vectored from all points.

I saw the Rennbahn coming up on my left, spotted the turn off to the right, braked, shifted down, and took the circular in a skid. It brought me beneath the overpass, facing the racetrack entrance ahead. The place was fenced, but a narrow road bordered it, and the dark bulk of trees loomed beyond. I killed the headlights. If the choppers had heat-seeking scanners, the woods wouldn't hide me. If not, they'd have trouble spotting the Mercedes before daylight. With the rain and poor visibility I had to slow to a walk. At the end of the track was a secondary road running perpendicular to it and, on the other side of that, woodland with bridle trails.

Even though it was growing lighter, I had to sense what was ahead more than see it in any detail. I chose what appeared to be the widest slot into the woods, knowing that much as I wanted to get rid of the Mercedes, I couldn't afford to get stuck. As I crawled along under the pine boughs, I listened to the expanding pursuit. Roadblocks were going up at all central points. The slingwing pilots were having trouble with visibility—the scud was down to the treetops and they were flying on the gauges.

The path had been no problem, but now it and trees were petering out, and I saw the lights of a car swing past ahead. It was moving slowly, and I could make out enough of its shape to know that it wasn't one of the hunters. I had no time to debate the issue. I moved. Lights on, siren blaring, I shot out of the woods and roared after the vehicle. The driver didn't argue; he pulled to the curb fast. I was out of the Mercedes faster.

An excited and frightened man stuck his head out of the Russian Volga's window. "What is it? What is it?" he was shouting.

"I need your car," I said.

"But I'm taking my wife to the hospital! She's very ill!" Through the window I saw the wife, sitting with her head lowered.

"You take my car." I yanked the door open. "This is an emergency too. Turn off your lights and do as you're told."

Over the rain I could hear a chopper, but I couldn't see its navigational lights.

I helped the man get his wife out of the Volga into the Mercedes. That was as much a good samaritan as I could afford to be. I left him standing in the road, stunned, looking at his new acquisition.

I knew there was a hospital only a few kilos away at Wuhlheide. I thought the chances were good they'd get there before being picked up.

CHAPTER 24

The Volga was not in the best of shape. It had probably never been in good shape. It was a helluva comedown
from a 450SE. I took it back down the bridle path, retracing my track to Treskow. I knew there would be a
major roadblock where it intersected with Rummelsburger. I took the first exit that came up, knowing I was going to have to get rid of the Volga as fast as I'd dumped
the Mercedes. Even if the couple did make it to the hospital without further interruption, the car would be spotted
swiftly.

There was a bit more traffic now, those going to work
early. I heard a patrol car go wailing down the Autobahn
toward the checkpoint as I moved along a street not unlike the one on which Jan Steuben lived. In this case,
however, there were houses only on the right side of the
street. On the left I could dimly see that a large construction operation was underway. A huge derrick stuck up in
the murk with a prehistoric look.

I saw the muddy entrance into the area, which was

fronted by a high brick wall, and took it. I switched off
the headlights. Dressed as I was, I had no chance of passing a checkpoint, wherever it was. Without a change of
clothes I was nailed down. Maybe there was a night
watchman who would lend me his. If not, from the size
and bulk of the site, it looked like a good place to tuck in
the Volga. It was.

The rain was slacking off and the light coming on fast.
In this case it helped, or I might have missed the culvert.
It was boxed in by cement walls and was already partially
covered over. It looked just wide enough to take the
Volga. I stopped at its edge and saw that its floor had a
nice downward slant. I put my back into it, and the Soviet
Volks went down the ramp and under the overhang.
There came the sound of scraping metal on concrete, and
a mating of sorts had occurred. Someone was going to
have a time trying to uncouple car and culvert.

I looked around in the gray mist to see if my parking
had disturbed anyone. All about were high piles of cinder-block prefab siding, the cellar structure and a rising
wall of what was going to be a large building, assorted
tools, and various elements of construction, with the derrick as the centerpiece. Close to it was a large van, serv-
ing as an office. There was no light in its windows, and it
was buttoned up tight. There was no cab attached to the
van, or I might have had a way out. Neither was there a
night watchman with whom I could change rank. Across
the street were a few dim houselights. I needed not only
a change of clothes, but also a hot cup of coffee. I'd been
separated from food for far too long. The thought of
breakfast headed me toward the domestic scene.

I didn't get very far. I don't know how the slingwing
found me—heat seeking device or what. He came out of
the sky muck with a clatter, skidding past the derrick's
reach, settling fast, coming around toward me.

There was a stack of waist high cinder blocks a few
feet away. I took them on the run, amidst a flight of bees,
killing bees, bits of the block peppering my hands as I

vaulted. The chopper flapped on over and I got a look at a goggled face staring down at me, trying to bring his AK-47 to bear.

I went back over the blocks and legged it to a more congested part of the site. I was crouched behind a wall as the chopper made its second swing. It went skittering past, looking for me. I knew I couldn't knock it down with a Luger. I knew, too, that the pilot would be in touch with ground control, and unless I could get out of the area fast, I was in for it.

I had only one choice. As he swung around toward me, I stood up, Wilhelmina in hand, and pretended to shoot at him.

The gunner was trying to get a shot at me as I dropped down and legged it in a crouch to the far end of the wall. At its end were a pair of cylinders, drainage pipes. They lay perpendicular to the wall, their ends in line with it. I went into the nearest in a dive and went down its short length on all fours.

The echo of the chopper's sound inside the pipe gave the impression that it was landing on my back. Not quite. As I had hoped, the pilot was settling down on the opposite side of the wall. I recognized the bird as a Hengstrom 5D, a two-place bubble job. From where I lay I could see its rotor blades slow to idling and hear the *whack-whack-whack* drowning out all other sound.

It was nearly daylight and although that wasn't saying much in the gray gloom, it was working against me. Time had nearly run out. I had to make a move; yet I forced myself to wait, crouching at the end of the pipe to see if the gunner would come looking. He didn't, and I knew it was time for the groundhog to come out and see if he could find his shadow.

No doubt, their control had told the two-man crew to sit tight and wait for reinforcements. Hanging over me might have been the safest course for them. But in the rain and scud and bad light and the derrick's reach, not to mention my taking potshots, it had been decided otherwise. A slingwing is great for pursuit over open terrain but not around an obstacle course. The gunner did not show.

I headed for the far end of the wall. Around its edge I took in the scene. The gunner had got out. He had his back to me at the moment, speaking into a walkie-talkie to either the pilot or home base. He was turning full circle as he spoke, his submachine gun cradled on his hip. He was too far distant to bring down with Wilhelmina. If I rushed him I'd never get there. There were some broken pieces of brick scattered around. Like little David, I chose my pieces with care.

Then I had another look. The gunner was attaching his radio to his belt. I stood clear and let fly.

The gray rock blended with the gray light. It arched and dropped as I sent another after it, and then a third. I don't know which made contact with one of the circling blades. I heard a thunk and a screech of metal, and I saw a part of one blade go winging away. Immediately the Hengstrom began to vibrate and chatter in protest, its blades out of balance.

The pilot wasn't sure what had happened to his bird. The gunner stood flatfooted, looking up at the harsh racketing sound, realizing something was sure as hell wrong. It was a frozen instant and all the time I had left to move. Over the agonized sound, and the pilot's momentary fumbling, I sprinted toward my would-be killer.

Just before I got to him he knew I was there. Head and shoulders started to swivel. I went down low, driving my head between his legs and then lifting up, thrusting his body high. He got off one shout of surprise, and then a rotor blade made contact with his head.

The sound was a kind of a wet *thunk*. The force of the blow knocked him off my shoulders. Good thing. He'd lost his head, and the result was messy. I scooped up his AK-47.

When the pilot saw the result of the action, he hit the panic button. He tried to take off. With one blade short and another undoubtedly bent, the chopper wasn't exactly aerodynamically sound. He got the Hengstrom up about ten feet, jiggling and bobbing like a yoyo not wanting to yo. Then it skidded violently to the left, tipping at the same time. The landing gear slammed into the wall, and the bubble, like a whirling Humpty Dumpty, fell on the other side with a spaced-out racket, pieces of flying blades singing through the drizzly morning air.

Through the same morning air, over the sound, I heard the wail of a fast-approaching siren. Reinforcements had arrived. I ran for the entrance to the site and had just about reached it when the helicopter blew up. Over my shoulder I glimpsed a miniature mushroom cloud being formed out of a stem of flame. The air was full of interchangeable parts.

I was at the entrance way as the gray patrol car was braking and swinging in.

I waved my arm, AK held high. "Hold it! Hold it! Halt!" I shouted.

The patrol car skidded to a stop. There were three of them in it. The flames from the chopper had half their attention. I had the other half.

"Get out here!" I ordered. "There are at least four of them. They're well armed."

"What happened, sir?" the driver said stupidly. "We heard there was only one."

"Get the hell out!" I gestured angrily. "And spread out!"

They moved to obey, and I thought I had it made. Then I heard the siren of the second car and saw another slingwing settling down to have a look.

"Contact him!" I said to the driver, pointing to the chopper. "Tell him to stay clear or he'll get what the other one got." He returned to do so, as I moved past the entrance into the street.

I signaled the approaching car to a stop. There were only two in it, a sergeant sitting next to the driver.

The sergeant had the window down. I gave him the

same quick information as the others and added, "I want you to take command. Pin them down, but don't try to move in on them, understand?"

"Yes, sir!" He was out of the car on the run, anxious to be number one.

I climbed into his seat. "Get moving!" I said, gesturing straight ahead.

CHAPTER 25

Bluff, of course, requires acceptance by those being bluffed that everything is as it should be. The flames from the crashed helicopter, and my appearing to be a major in the security forces, AK in hand, were the high cards that I'd held. But as any poker player will tell you, there comes a time when you're going to be called. I knew that time had nearly arrived.

The volume on the radio was up full. A voice was blasting, giving orders to ground and aerial patrols to converge on the point we had just departed.

"Turn that damn thing down!" I ordered, reaching for the knob and doing it myself.

The driver was a meaty type, thickbodied, thickfaced, and thickheaded—but not all that thickheaded. He was beginning to take a closer look at me. He was beginning to wonder why we were headed away from the point of contact.

"I want to stop at the checkpoint on Rummelsburger," I said. "Is this as fast as you can drive?" It was daylight now, as light as it was going to be, and there was traffic ahead and behind. It had begun to rain hard again.

"Sir, we can contact the control, if you like," Beefy said, testing.

"Don't you think I know that, you oaf? Let's move, move!"

He hit the siren and the accelerator. "I should report my location, sir." He reached for the mike on the pedestal.

"I'll do the reporting. Gimme that." My hand was quicker than his.

I was counting on our running into a traffic jam. The road we were on fed into the Autobahn where the checkpoint would be. We would be boxed in, and I'd order Beefy to go on foot and bring back Captain Bielfeld. When he'd departed, I'd depart too and commandeer a car going in the opposite direction and try to work my way north, possibly taking another S-Bahn ride.

My goal now was the U.S. Embassy. It was a lousy plan, but I was out of options.

Beefy scotched it and called my bluff, coming up with a P-38 in his left hand. "Major, you don't move, or I shoot," he said, face flushed, not altogether sure but willing to risk it. He slowed, pulling toward the curb, knowing he couldn't very well relieve me of the mike while his other hand was on the wheel.

"What the hell do you think you're doing!" I shouted, knowing he knew damn well what he was doing but wanting the roar of my voice and outrage to shake him up a bit.

He couldn't keep his eyes on me entirely, and as we came to a stop, he took a quick glance ahead. I made my move.

I backhanded him with a chop to what there was of his neck. The blow brought a retching gargle out of him, and as his head went back and his wheel hand went to the relief of his throat, I went for his gun.

He might have been hurting in the wind pipe, but that wasn't enough to bother the rest of him.

My idea was to jam the barrel against him and pull the trigger. He'd been through that routine before. He yanked his wrist upward and reached to get an arm around my neck. He missed but got the steel claw of his hand on my shoulder, then on my throat. Even though the windows were fogged with condensation, I knew if our necking match went on for more than a few seconds it was going to bring an uninvited audience.

I let him think he had me, and as he brought his weight around from the wheel, pressing me against the door, I began to make strangling sounds.

I was still holding on to the P-38, keeping the barrel up and away. He had a nasty leer on his hamburger face as he tightened his grip on my throat with his right hand and began a yanking motion with his left.

Hugo came out of the raincoat pocket easily enough. I didn't want to make too much of a mess, but I slashed his wrist and got some much-needed air. He hauled back his right with a shout of shock and pain. He had more coming.

I laid Hugo's point against his jugular and said, "Drop it on the floor."

He had *some* brains. He did as he was told.

"Put your hands on the wheel."

"My arm! My wrist! I must stop the blood, *bitte!*"

"You do as I say or you'll be losing a lot more!"

He obeyed. His hat had fallen off. It was on the floor between us. "You'll need your hat," I said. "Pick it up."

I brought Wilhelmina into view. There was terror in his shoe-button eyes. *"Bitte! Bitte!"* he choked.

"Do as I say."

As he did as I said, I tested the thickness of his skull with the Luger's butt. I put away Wilhelmina and added the P-38 to my arsenal. Then I turned up the volume and learned that everything was being zeroed in on the con-

struction site. Before getting out of the car I made a mess
of the transmitter.

When I stepped out into the rain I was a furious officer
of the MFS, giving his stupid driver hell for breaking
down in such a place.

Because of the checkpoint at the intersection, there was
no traffic coming up from the Autobahn. There was only
the bumper-to-bumper lane, heading down toward it.
Since they were Germans, and Germans under a Nazi-like
rule, no one thought to do a ninety-degree turn into the
scattering of single-lane side roads. No one, that is, but a
Saab 99LE with Swedish diplomatic plates.

The driver was having a tough time of it. The car in
front was stopped. The car in back didn't want to retreat
an inch, even if the result would bring a gain of several
meters.

I lent a hand, rapping on the driver's window, gesturing
for it to back up. I did the same to the car behind it. The
jockeying offered enough space for the four-door Saab to
pull out of the line. As it moved to do so, swinging
toward the side road, I stepped in front of it and came
around to the window, knocking on it.

Through the half-fogged glass, I could see a kind of Viking. The window went down, and she said rudely, "What
do you want?"

"Is that any way to thank a benefactor? I'd like a lift.
My car's broken down." I gestured to the traffic bent
around the gray hulk.

She was a natural blond, blue-eyed, full-lipped, big-
breasted, and out of sorts. "I'm not going your way," she
said, and began cranking up the window.

"Yes you are." I smiled. I went around the front again,
half-expecting her to run me down, and got in on the passenger's side.

"You see here!" she spat angrily. "I'm not one of your
liberated subjects! You—!"

"Of course you're not. You're Beowulf's daughter, and if you want to get out of here you'd better go now, because in a couple of minutes the whole area will be closed up." I pointed to the side road.

Glaring furiously, she slammed in the clutch, and we shot ahead. Getting an inside closer look at her was better than an outside rainy one. She was big boned, and her features were the kind that look good on a stage. She wore a soft wide-brimmed felt hat and a London Fog coat and had an open-air Scandinavian aura about her.

"Terrible morning," I said.

"Would you mind telling me what's going on? Road blocks everywhere. Why can't you people relax? Why do you have to hunt each other like wolves?"

"I'm relaxed," I said, sitting back.

She gave me another glare. "You're getting my car soaking wet. Where does this road go?"

"Are you headed for your embassy?"

"I am not! I've been at the embassy all right. I'm headed home to bed."

"Nice morning for it."

"Where do you want to get off? I live in Fredrichsfeld."

"That will be fine. Tell me, were there road blocks in the center of the city?"

"Everywhere! I've been circling around for a half hour trying to avoid them."

"Why? Are you a spy?"

"Have you ever been caught in one of your stupid checks? You saw what was happening back there. It takes hours!"

"If it hadn't been for me, Fraulein, you'd still be back there."

"All you wanted was a lift."

"So we both got something out of it. Incidentally, I don't know your name."

"Is that necessary?"

"It helps. I want to thank you."

"Karen Pettersen. And who are you?"

"Major Nick."

"Nick? That's an odd name."

"A rose by any other."

"Oh Lord, look!"

We were coming out of a housing district into a neighborhood center. Ahead was a cluster of mustard-colored Russian Jeeps on either side of the road. Vopos were checking pedestrians as well as automotive traffic.

"Stop right here," I said.

The way I said it brought her eyes back to mine. They were perceptive eyes, steady, direct, almost masculine.

"Now," I added. "One question, one quick answer," I said in English. "Do you like East Germans?"

She studied my face. "I hate the stupid bastards," she replied in German.

"With your diplomatic plates you should be able to pass that check without too much trouble. With these fogged up windows, no one can see in the back, particularly if the doors are locked. I'll be in the back."

"Who the hell *are* you!" The Swedish inflection in German made me want to hear her say it in English—Ooo the ell are yew!

"Nick," I said, easing myself over the seat into the back. I sat on the floor and took out Wilhelmina and the P-38. There was a large beach blanket on the seat. I tried to drape it around me.

The car got underway. "You've got a helluva nerve," she said, but I liked the way she said it.

"If it comes to trouble, you can say I forced you."

"You can bet on that!"

"Get us through and I'll buy you a cup of coffee."

"If I get us through, I'll make you one. Now be still."

It was a thin business, and I didn't like risking her pretty Swedish neck. The beach blanket was a pastel blue, almost the same color as the car's interior. If the door stayed shut and no one got too nosy, I'd enjoy her coffee. If the door opened I would have no choice but to go out shooting.

The Saab slowed to a crawl. I heard her crank down the window. She began beeping the horn impatiently. "Get out of my way!" she called. "Get out of my way!"

The Saab jerked to a stop.

"Guten tag, Fraulein," a voice said politely.

"Tag!" She replied. "Will you please let me pass? I must be at the Swedish Embassy by seven o'clock. I am the ambassador's personal secretary. Here are my papers. Now please!"

"But Fraulein, your embassy is on Unter den Linden, and—"

"I know where my embassy is, sir! And I know how difficult it is to get there with you people stopping traffic at every corner."

"You are Fraulein Karen Pettersen?"

"You can read it, and you can see it from the photograph."

"Do you have your green card, Fraulein Pettersen?"

"It's right there, and you know it!"

"Ahh, yes. Very well." I heard her taking back the papers. "Now may we have the key to the trunk?"

"This is damned ridiculous!"

"Sorry, Fraulein. Orders."

"The trunk is open."

One thing I would never hide in is a car trunk. The inspection was swift. I heard the top go up and the top go down.

Someone tried to open the back door, and the polite one said, "Fraulein, may we have a look in the back?"

Her voice was laced with Arctic chill, not railing now but low and throaty. "You either let me pass this instant, or I'll have Ambassador Swenson report this insult to your foreign minister with whom he is having breakfast this morning at seven o'clock, providing I am present to make a record!"

The silence was very brief, but during it I made sure that my legs weren't going to get tangled when I went out. Two-gun Carter, his moment was swift.

"If you take Hauptstrasse, it will—"

She cut off his voice by cranking up the window and throwing the clutch in. We began to move.

Neither of us spoke until she was cruising. "You know, Karen," I said, "I don't doubt that you're the best secretary that ever was, but as an actress and a life saver, you'll always have my vote."

Her laughter was a warm, sensual sound. "But I'm not a secretary! I'm a political-affairs officer. And as for saving lives, it wasn't your life I was saving, it was mine."

"Well, thank you for saving yours. And how far is that cup of coffee?"

CHAPTER 26

Karen's apartment was a duplex in a newly built complex. When East Berlin had become the officially recognized capital of the DDR in '73, there had been some frantic construction work to take care of the sudden influx of foreign nationals, even though most of the ambassadorial types lived in West Berlin.

The building was a fan affair with the apartments projecting like fins from a central core, each flat ending in ceiling-height windows. From the twelfth floor the view was toward Frankfurter Alle. Even in the gray murk I could see a road block at Fredrichfelde, and I could make another one out at the Litchenberg intersection. Even Karen wouldn't be able to bluff her way through that kind of security. By now all traffic in the city was bottled up.

"Well, do you always get half-undressed for a cup of coffee?"

I turned around, grinning at her. "It all depends. In

this case, I didn't have time to get fully dressed when I left my hotel."

She stood tray in hand, examining me as I faced her stripped to the waist, returning her gaze. She was tall and nicely proportioned, her breasts thrusting her blouse out proudly. She moved gracefully, like an athlete, with contained control. "Well, I'm glad you were able to put on something," she chuckled.

"You wouldn't have an extra shirt, would you?"

She set down the tray and straightened, licking her thumb. "Nothing I wear would fit you, but I might find something. Come have your coffee and kroeller."

I had my coffee and kroeller. I was in need of both. "Excellent coffee, Karen. I knew it would be."

"What do I call you, Tarzan or something?" We sat facing each other across a handsome low boy.

"You call me Nick, but drop the title."

I had examined the room for bugs, but I knew that the host country made it a standard practice to include them in the construction plans behind the walls and in the ceilings.

I pointed. "Do you have many neighbors?"

"We did have some, but they're gone now."

"Sure?"

"Positive. You know the kind of tinsel you have on a Christmas tree? You blow it into the wall like insulation, and—"

"It sets up a shield that puts up a hum in the neighbor's ear."

"Exactly. Who are you, anyway?"

"I'm better than I was, and I'll have another cup of coffee, please."

"And then what?" She poured.

"And then I want you to call the American Embassy."

"There's no tinsel in the telephone. I thought you must be an American. Only an American would behave like you."

"I hope that's a compliment. Ask for Frank Emory."

"The commercial attaché."

"All the better if you know him."

"Then what?"

"Then I'll talk to him. He won't be at the embassy before nine. They'll give you his home number."

"I happen to have it. I don't know why I'm doing all this for you."

"We're on the same side."

"No, I'm neutral."

"But you think East Germans are bastards, so that puts us on the same side."

"Yes, but why should I risk my neck?"

"Very pretty neck. I'll call you Karen Swan Neck."

"I don't know if I like that. How long do you expect to stay here?"

"That depends."

"On what?" Her mouth was long and full, and her underlip was very full.

"On Frank Emory and those road blocks out there."

"You're trying to reach the American Embassy."

"Something like that."

"And you want him to come and pick you up. He'll be stopped at all those road blocks too, and he won't get through the way I did."

"Let's give him a call."

His home number did not answer. He was not at the embassy. At this hour, no one was there but the Marine guard.

"Now what?" Karen put down the phone.

"You wanted to get some sleep."

We were standing very close together. The way her hair was cut in a straight line across her forehead, it looked as though her face were framed by a Viking helmet. She had a primitive Norse look. "Loki," I said.

"Help me with the bed." It was a Murphy-type affair, tucked into an alcove. It was large and inviting. We faced each other across it.

"How good a lover are you?" she asked with a chuckle, starting to unbutton her blouse.

"Shall we find out?" I had less to take off than she, but I wasn't much ahead of her in getting undressed completely.

Statuesque might be one word. *Magnificent* might be another. Her breasts were large but not pendulous. Her waist was slim, her hips wide and tapering to long, agile legs. She had a solid and glowing body, firm and strong.

I could ask myself—or Hawk could ask me—what the hell I was doing making love at a time like this. And the answer was, I couldn't think of anything better to do at a time like this. For the moment, I was trapped. I could no more get to my escape point than fly without benefit of aircraft. For Karen to start burning up bugged telephone wires in an attempt to make contact with anyone else in the U.S. Embassy would only attract attention. Emory was my embassy contact, but if I couldn't reach him then I had to try to get back across the Spree. And the way things were, I couldn't try it for another hour, at least. So . . .

She was not a woman who enjoyed preliminaries, although my tongue on her nipples not only made them erect but brought her head back as well. From the way her hands gripped me I knew she was not the tender, romantic type. She was the kind that you had to conquer, in a kind of war of the sexes. If you didn't win, she'd have only contempt for you. At the same time, all her efforts would be to defeat you.

I entered her like a jackhammer. She rose to meet my thrusts, trying to set the rhythm. Her face was expressionless, eyes wide, mouth shut. After some tossing about I set the pace, steady and hard, not too fast. She was there with every stroke, and the way she was there, inside and out, was fiercely elemental. She was out to suck the marrow from my bones. We went on and on. When she blinked I increased the stroke. I was beginning to think she was going to win the contest. Then suddenly I got to her.

Her eyes closed, her head arched back, her mouth opened with a long, shuddering sigh. She began twisting, breasts thrust against my chest, hands gripping me. I increased the pace and power of my drive. She moaned, rocking her head from side to side. I knew I was almost to the point of no return, when she cried out, "Oh, God! Now! Now! Now!"

I gave her my all through her orgasm, and it was like riding an earthquake. Then as she opened her eyes I let myself go, and the force of it made her come again.

When we got our wind back she spoke first. "I don't know who you are or where you're going, but do you really have to go?"

"Duty, Flavia, duty. Would you like a cigarette?"

"So old-fashioned." She shook her head.

"It has its points."

She gave me a throaty laugh.

"And now it's time to get to work, love," I said.

"Oh, must you!" She tried to hold me down.

"I'll take a raincheck."

"But it's raining now. It's going to rain all day."

"It'll be raining again. I'll get the phone for you."

As I had suspected, Emory, the ambassador, and every officer of consequence had gone to West Berlin the night before to be on hand for the President's arrival.

"You see, you don't have to go." She put down the phone, coming at me in all her Viking nakedness.

"I do, and I need your help."

When we left Karen's apartment I was dressed somewhat differently. I was wearing a dark blue turtleneck shirt, unknowingly donated by her friend the baron. Thanks to her hair coloring, my black hair had turned a muddy blond. To cap it, I wore the baron's driving hat, a colorful red-checked affair, and my pants were a pair of snug-fitting corduroys, ownership not recalled.

Karen had entered into the spirit of the thing, but she was protesting, even as we drove out of the complex garage, that I could have at least made love to her once more.

The time had come to get serious. It was eight o'clock. The radio had been broadcasting an alert for a murderer. The description was close. The road blocks were still tying up traffic on the main arteries.

Karen had a map of the city, and with it I had plotted a course by secondary roads to the ring, entering it just above Warschauer. I'd kiss her goodbye there, and she'd go on to her embassy. I had decided to do the driving. There were two ways to look at it. If she drove I'd have more flexibility if our bluff was called. But I didn't want our bluff called, and the chances were better that it wouldn't be, with me at the wheel.

She caught the psychology of it and added a finishing touch to our roles by putting an official diplomatic sticker with a DDR seal on the window. I didn't like putting her neck on the line. But at the moment necks weren't that important. More than that, I saw that she was the kind of Norsewoman who would dare anything, the kind who'd make a good AXE agent. Unlike most women, she didn't ask unnecessary questions. She got the message fast, and that was enough.

"I really should be sleeping, you know," she said, laughing at me, as we drove out of the garage.

Our luck held until we got to the intersection at Marx Alle and Boxhagener. It was impossible to get around it. We knew we were for it when the traffic ahead slowed suddenly and we were in a line.

"Know your part?" I said.

"Perfectly." She moved over next to me, put her arm through mine, and laid her head on my shoulder. "I may have to contain myself."

"Don't overdo it."

There were no slingwings in the sky now. The overcast was sitting on the building tops. The windshield wipers clanked. The rain came down. Through the mess I saw two guards approach the car ahead. One went to the driver's window; the other checked the passenger's side, opening the door and leaning in. He got the keys and went to the trunk. The one on the driver's side got the documentation. Going through it he managed to get the handful of papers thoroughly soaked before handing them back. The sedan moved away slowly, and I pulled up between the checkers.

I cranked down the window. *"Guten tag.* We are in a hurry, Captain," I said, grinning. "We are getting married this morning."

Karen kissed me on the neck and looked out at him. The door opened on her side, and a wet, surly face came dripping in. "Your keys, *bitte."*

Karen pulled her legs up. "Oh! You're getting me all wet! Get out of here!"

"You don't need any keys," I said, suddenly annoyed. "Everything is open. And stop dripping all over everything!"

The head went out, and the door slammed.

"What's the matter with him?" I said to my guard.

"He'd rather be inside. May I have your papers?"

"You want our marriage certificate?" I smiled again.

"Darling, maybe he'd like to come to the wedding." She smiled at him, hugging my arm.

"What's going on, anyway?" I said. "Why are you stopping us? We are diplomatic and we're late. The ambassador is going to marry us."

"At this time of day?" The Vopo was mildly interested.

"Yes. He's got to go over to West Berlin to be present when the American President comes."

The door opener had made sure we were alone in the car and had nothing in the trunk. Now he joined his equally soaked comrade, anxious to move on.

"Darling, show the captain who you are," I said.

"But he can see who I am!" She straightened up, pointing. "We are Swedes, not Germans, and we are diplomatic. See, there." She pointed. "We have that from your security. It means we are not to be stopped like this at all. Isn't that so?"

"The man's only doing his duty, Karen."

"But Torgle. . . !"

"Come on," the door opener said. "Let them pass. We'll never get through here."

And so with a soggy assist, we two lovers passed.

"I'm going to stop at the S-Bahn," I said as we cleared the checkpoint.

"I'll kiss you goodbye and cry a little," she sighed, grinning.

"I'm sorry it's been so short. Go directly to your embassy. They may check up."

"I'm not that far away," she said, ignoring my instructions. "I can come to the West any time."

"I'll give you a call."

"You'd better." She wrapped her arm around mine again and kissed my neck.

The S-Bahn station at Warschauer had a fair-sized crowd around it, trying to get in out of the rain. It couldn't be done without first being checked by a four-man patrol at the entrance doors. It was a helluva way for someone to start the day.

I pulled up on the other side of the street. "Parting is such sweet sorrow, Viking lady," I said, "but this is farewell for now."

For the first time there was a look of concern, almost pain, on her face. "Nick, when you arrive where you're going, call me. Please call me."

"You bet." We kissed. I was momentarily sorry the circumstances hadn't been different. We could have had a lot of fun.

"Promise," she said, as I got out.

"Promise. Now honey, get the hell out of here, and thanks for the ride."

I blew her a kiss as the Saab did a 180 and hissed away.

CHAPTER 27

Staying close to building fronts, ducking into one as I
sensed a patrol was coming around a corner, I avoided
contact until I turned in to Rotherstrasse, two blocks from
the alley.

He was up on a roof across from me, AK at the ready.
"You down there!" he shouted. "Where the hell do you
think you're going!"

I didn't answer. I sprinted across the street, angling for
the corner, knowing I'd be out of his line of fire—if I
made it.

He opened up, and the pavement began to sing around
me, stone splinters spraying. I made the corner, and like a
good soldier he stopped shooting and began blowing his
whistle.

Things were down to basics. I ran with Wilhelmina in
hand, the P-38 in reserve. A siren started to wail. A two-
man team was trotting toward me as I rounded the next
corner. Their instant of surprise made the difference. I

fired four times, charging them, before they could get their fingers moving. One went down shooting at the ground. The other sank onto his knees, gripping his gut. As I ran past I scooped up the kneeling man's weapon.

I had the alley in sight when I heard the car behind me, coming full out. I spun around and dropped to one knee, holding my fire until the vehicle was in close. Someone was leaning out the window, having a go at me. I replied with a quick burst and saw the windshield disappear.

The Ziv swerved violently, went up over the curb, changed course, and slammed into a building front. I didn't wait for the sound to die.

From several blocks down the street more company began to arrive as an open Jeep carrier took the corner at an unsafe speed. The entrance to the alley looked like the pass at Dinant—open to he who could get there first. I made it by a whisker amid a great deal of unfriendly noise and a hail of stone fragments.

The driver of the carrier was smart enough not to stop at the alley's entrance, which gave me a chance to cover some additional ground before the troops arrived. Two did at the same time and let go with hosing bursts.

I would have been well crocheted if I hadn't known about the pile of rubble about a quarter of the way along the tube. I went down behind it just as they opened up. In the bad light, they paused for a second to check the effect of their aim. I spelled it out for them with return fire. The one with the grenade in his hand fell, grabbing his knee. His buddy jumped out of sight.

I didn't debate whether his retreat was a result of my action or because the pin had been pulled on the grenade. It must have been the latter, because it went off as I was racing for the manhole cover.

Above me I could hear the voice on the roof calling, and then a shouted, "He's in the alley between us!"

Marvelous deduction. I let off a burst at the building

parapet on my left just to prove that the man was right
and to keep them cautious in exploring the point. Someone began shooting again from the alley entrance. I hit the
ground, sliding along in the puddled muck on my belly,
reaching out to grab the home plate of the cover. The
way I was sucking in air, I didn't need to practice deep
breathing. It took a couple of hefty yanks to get the cover
raised. I snaked in behind it and lowered myself on the
ladder. All I wanted was the flippers; they could keep the
rest.

Someone had zeroed in on the raised cover, and it began to zing and clang under the hammering. Bingo night
in the shooting gallery. On the roof to my left a marks-
man tried to get the angle and started making rubble of
the rubble. I took in extra air and pulled down the trap.
In my last glance upward I spotted a grenade thrower in
the act.

With the heavy rain, I knew the drain would be filled,
its contents moving swiftly. I used the ARV to prove the
point. Then to save time I dropped from the top of the
ladder into the swilling stew. Its current gave me a fast
ride and flushed me into the Spree with all the other flotsam. With my remaining air, I stayed deep and swam
hard for the west bank. I knew the only chance I had was
to cross fast. If they managed to box me in, I was finished.

I surfaced in a lovely patch of fog. For a moment I
thought the Spree might be wearing a blanket of it. No
such luck. One careful stroke and I was out of it.

The air was full of the sound of sirens and the heavy
beat of diesels. The flat roofs of the buildings that lined
the east bank were decked with Vopos trying to spot me.
A patrol boat was idling in close by the bridge abutment,
the comrades above shouting down instructions.

I sank carefully and pulled for the shore. It wasn't far,
and before I went under I noted that the East-side action
had attracted West-side interest. Cars were stopping and

people were coming down quickly to line the bank.

When I had submerged I had seen no patrol boat near me. Somehow in the gray light with its gray color I had missed it. Now I could hear the sound of its rapid approach. I knew damn well it had spotted me.

All it had to do was wait until I came up . . . like a dead fish. Its crew was impatient. The first concussion grenade was far enough away so that it merely drove a harpoon through my head via my ears. No one heard me shout or saw me thrashing over the effect. I knew the next one would kill me.

It would have, had my head remained under. I surfaced, not like Moby Dick, but blowing blood out of my mouth and nose, P-38 in hand, determined that I was going to leave them something to remember me by. I knew also that whatever happened here was going to spread all over West Berlin like wildfire, and that the message might come through that security around the President would have to be made so tight that he couldn't afford to make the stop. Maybe it was a forlorn hope. But it was all I had left.

The hunters were bearing down on me at slow speed. There was a lookout on the bow, AK at the ready. He didn't expect me to be armed or good enough to shoot him from the water.

I fired twice, and then there were two of us thrashing around in the Spree. They had to stop and pick him up, and they couldn't let go with any more grenades until they did. But now I was starting to draw fire from the roof tops.

As I went under again I could hear voices shouting encouragement from the West bank. I knew I didn't have much push left. I could hear the diesels of other boats coming on the run, coming in for the kill.

I was so damn close, but the bastards claimed the whole canal. I didn't have a prayer unless I got out of it. Weakness and no air forced me to the top. At first I

"No. Interesting case, though. Any others?" I asked the sergeant.

"He was the last, sir."

I turned away from the desk where the report lay, relieved on one count. Although the fire had exposed the fake rear of the building and the area where Kraemer had his communication equipment, I knew the police had found nothing in the rubble to arouse suspicion of Kraemer's secret activities. Fire brought automatic disintegration through the use of CLYYB, an AXE–perfected acid that left nothing but unidentifiable ashes.

Had the equipment or any part of it been found intact, it would have brought immediate attention by West Berlin security, regardless of their seeming lack of interest. I could be thankful for AXE R&D. But all I could chalk up for my progress so far was a growing number of bodies, the growing suspicion of counterproductive action by an ally, and a date with a college instructor. It added up to zilch.

On the plus side, N12's body was not in cold storage. Old John might still be up and about somewhere. I had noted the unclaimed corpses, late of the *Stadtbad,* and the fact that neither Horst Lutz nor any of his murderers had been added to the refrigerator lockers. Count your blessings while you may.

"Shall we go?" I said.

Before I headed back to the hotel I joined Wehner in his car for a cigarette.

"After you've talked to Fraulein Raeder you can call me at the usual number, if you like," he said.

"We'll see, Paul."

"I have done you some small favors, Nick. Do me this one, *bitte.*"

He was right, of course, and until now, no questions asked. But it didn't change a damn thing. Something was off the track with Paul Wehner.

CHAPTER 10

The rain had slacked off as I swung the Volvo onto Leibnizstrasse. Hilma Liebfraumilch, or whatever her name was, was to call my room at exactly ten. I had time to spare and moved along on the wet pavement at moderate speed. There was no evidence I had been tailed. There was really no need for it. Both sides knew where I was staying. Lola for the opposition, Paul Wehner for the BND.

As soon as I'd finished with Fraulein Raeder, I was clearing out, taking up a new residence elsewhere. The Osdorf was beginning to take on all the charm and privacy of the New York Port Authority bus station at five in the afternoon.

I saw that the ramp going down into the hotel garage was blocked by what looked like a black Maria. I knew Zitor wouldn't allow the entrance to be jammed, principally because it served as both *ingang* and *ausgang*. I slowed, as though planning to pull in and park on the tree-shaded street just short of the entrance. As I eased in

64

thought I was coming up in another lucky patch of fog. But fog doesn't cackle and chirp and, according to Carl Sandburg, travel on webbed feet. I eased my head up in the middle of the swan flock. I'd always heard that swans were ugly customers, beautiful to look at but mean to fool with. Maybe they are to the mindless trolls on the East side. But in this case they gave me a story to tell my grandchildren—if I should live so long. They saved my life, and they knew what they were doing. They hemmed me in on all sides, concealed my head with their wings, and, raising a helluvan annoyed cackle, maneuvered me to the dock inlet that was their regular nesting point.

The patrol boats circled in a kind of fury, searching for me, disturbing the water with more grenades. The Vopos on the roofs kept shouting and pointing, seeing my head in every piece of garbage.

The crowd was now large, spread along the West bank. They were shaking their fists and calling insults across the water. The swans moved me along, clucking their own orders. There were a number of people on the dock, watching the action, paying no attention to the birds. "Ach, I'm afraid they got him," a voice above me said.

"Bloody swine!" said another.

"Murderers!" shouted a woman.

The crowd took up the cry and began to chant it. The word echoed across the canal, bouncing off the buildings.

"Get out of here, you no-good bastards!" a voice above me called.

"Where do you suppose he's gone?" someone questioned.

"I'll tell you," I said quietly, "if you'll just give me a hand and get me the hell out of here before they know it and start shooting."

There was a moment on the dock when the only sound was the agreement voiced by the swans.

Then hands were reaching for mine. I was conscious of

being surrounded by human bodies in the place of white birds, of being rushed from the bank toward a police van. But I never got a chance to say thanks before the effects of the grenade laid me out.

CHAPTER 28

I was down on the bottom of the Spree, pinned by Karen. My air had run out. Time had run out. I had to break free!

Even while I was out cold, my unconscious was telling me to get the hell back into the world of the living. I don't know how I got loose from the weight of her. I surfaced and opened my eyes. I was in a hospital room. I was being watched over, not by a nurse, but by a West German policeman.

He wasn't watching me as closely as he was reading a copy of the *Berliner Morganpost*. As I willed myself out of whatever I'd been sedated with, I read the upside-down banner headline: U.S. PRESIDENT TO VISIT.

On the wall over the door a clock said 11:45. It was still raining. It had to be today, it couldn't be tomorrow. I had to get the damned fog out of my head.

"Has he arrived?" I said.

The policeman jerked and nearly tore the paper,

jumping up from his chair. "Ahh! You're awake!" he said stupidly.

"Has the President arrived?" I repeated.

"Oh, *jah! Jah!* He—!"

"I want to know something else—has there been a mass escape from East Berlin?"

He showed me all his teeth. "*Jah, jah!* You bet, the biggest in twelve years! Two great things at once. We have—!"

"Shut up and listen to me carefully!" I ordered. "You have a commanding officer. Bring him here as quickly as you can or get him on the telephone for me."

"He-he's not here! He's not at headquarters. Everyone is on duty. What do you want?"

"I want some clothes, and I want some help. It's a matter of saving the President's life."

Had he not known that I was an escapee from the East myself, he might have required more convincing. But on the other hand, Berlin police by the very nature of their location have a built-in capability for reacting to the bizarre.

His name was Ernst, and he was no fool. He didn't argue with me about the state of my health, physical or mental. He got me a pair of slacks, a shirt, and a pair of shoes and socks. He also returned Wilhelmina and Hugo.

While I dressed I filled him in as much as necessary. He believed the forty-eight freedom seekers were in protective custody, although there was some rumor that one of them was missing.

He brought me word from the nurses watching TV in the hall that the President had finished his exchange of remarks at Rathaus Schöneberg and was now on his way to the Wall to visit Checkpoint Charlie. There, with other dignitaries, he would mount the observation stand from which he could see and be seen from beyond the Wall. He was scheduled to give a brief speech on youth and brotherhood. Unlike Joshua, he would not bring the walls down. The media boys would have to figure out whether the act was for the cause of *détente,* resistance, or both. It could be they'd be writing about neither. Murder would make everything else academic.

Before we departed the hospital I tried a call and so did Ernst. Mine was to U.S. military headquarters in Dalheim. The best I could raise was a sergeant who would go looking for a captain. There was no time.

First by walkie-talkie, and then as we drove out of the hospital grounds in his Jeep, Ernst tried to raise his own headquarters. Security was too busy protecting the President to listen to incoming calls that might save his life.

My head ached furiously. I was groggy—more a reaction to something some German Dr. Kildare had socked me with than the effect of the concussion grenade. Whatever the cause, I had to shake free of it.

While Ernst, looking lean and hungry, leaned on the horn as we shot down Bülows to Yorckstrasse, I reloaded Wilhelmina with some spare shells he had.

The crowds were growing heavier, and I knew we'd never get through Mehring Platz at the Friedrichstrasse junction. "Cut over onto Stressmann," I said. "Then go over Anhalter."

"We can get much closer at Mehring. We'll go on foot from there." Ernst had the habit of throwing back his head to get a long blond cowlick out of his eye.

"Ernst," I said, and my tone brought a quick glance, "you do as I say. I want you to drop me at the corner of Anhalter and Wilhelm. Then you go down to Mehring and make contact with the first security officer you can spot. You tell him the President has been set up for an assassination attempt, to get him out of the area at once. Whatever happens, he's got to be kept off that reviewing stand."

"You think they'd shoot him from the other side?" He gave me a look of disbelief.

"I think you can go faster if you try."

He tried, and I tried to raise someone on his police radio. It was like the standard scene from the old movie with the man on the ground trying to raise the plane that had already crashed. No response.

We came into Stresemann at an angle, and I wondered for a second whether Ernst was planning a billiard shot, with the Jeep as the cue ball and a building front as the side cushion. The street was two blocks from Friedrich-strasse and roughly parallel to it. For that reason it was empty, which was a small break. Anhalter was a right turn, and at its far corner, where it met Wilhelm, I'd be bailing out.

I knew the fastest way for me to reach the point of festivities was via Hilma's underground route to the tunnel. I'd go through the hole in the wall and up to Lutz's flat. From the storeroom off it, I'd be looking down on the reviewing stand. From there I could attract plenty of attention.

As my mind pictured the spot, something went click inside the frame, and the picture froze. I saw the piled books, the stacked cartons, the concave window, and the smaller window concealed by more boxes. It was all very similar to photographs I had seen in N12's file of a book bindery in Texas where another presidential assassin had taken aim. It was the perfect setup, with the escape route laid out—back down the tunnel to the East!

"Stop here!"

As Ernst complied, he shouted, "They're already at Checkpoint Charlie!" which was exactly what a radio announcer was proclaiming.

"Get down to Mehring! Find somebody!" was my farewell instruction as I began to run up the street hoping I could find the spot I'd been led to blindfolded by Hilma's boys.

The unhappy guard who had been placed at the below-street entrance helped me. He heard my approach and came up to get a piece of the action. I gave him a quick piece. He had time to look alarmed, open his mouth, and start to unsling his weapon. Then he went back down the steps head first. I hoped that I hadn't broken his jaw and that the hard landing wouldn't cave in his skull. I also hoped there weren't going to be guards at the tunnel entrance. It would be normal to have them posted there. But this wasn't a normal day.

There were no guards, but in the dim light I could see that the tunnel opening had been sealed with a makeshift wooden partition.

Charging up the long flights to Lutz's former hideaway gave me a fair indication of my condition. Lousy. It was like being under the Spree. I couldn't find enough air to feed my lungs. My head was full of glass splinters. The growing roar I heard sounded more like the surf than a wildly enthusiastic crowd.

The door to Lutz's flat was locked from the inside. I felt the chill of its meaning as a shot from Wilhelmina shattered the mechanism. I knew why the three had come that night, not just to get rid of Lutz, but also to leave a weapon hidden in the storeroom for the hit man. My forlorn hope that the windows of the storeroom would be filled with spectators had died stillborn. There would be security men on all the rooftops, but no one would be permitted above the ground floor. I knew this as I kicked open the door and stood clear long enough to see that no one was waiting for me in the flat.

The double doors to the storeroom were closed. They were the sliding type, old-fashioned. I slid one open and jumped to the opposite side. All that came at me was the roar of the crowd.

I went into the room in a dive, coming down on all fours behind a stack of books. In midflight I'd seen that the windows fronting the street was empty. I had been almost sure there would be one spectator . . . with a rifle.

What the hell! For an instant my mind was in a black hole. Then I was up and in three steps was in flight again.

I cleared the shoulder-high cartons, walling the odd cupola window, and came down on my man. He was kneeling on one leg, the barrel of his rifle, with silencer attached, pointing down at an angle.

If he had had time, he could have had me cold. But time had run out. The target he'd been programmed for was in his sights. From some other world, I knew that the crowd had gone silent. Funneled through a PA system, I could hear the familiar voice of the President.

I plowed into the sharpshooter as his finger tightened on the trigger. The gun made a heavy thunking sound. Then I was fighting to kill, aware that in that other world all had gone momentarily silent.

Although I had the advantage of surprise, in my condition the man from Dallas had it on me in strength and speed. That left me with guile. But he had that too. I had lost Wilhelmina as we had gone down in a tangle. Then it was knees to balls, thumb to eye, hands to throat.

I tried to bring Hugo to bear. He anticipated me and caught my wrist, and we thrashed eyeball to eyeball. His were red where they should have been white, the irises cobalt. His face was seamed and pitted, and his bared teeth protruded. His breath made a tearing sound—or was it my breath? He stank of sweat and cigar smoke. There wasn't time to go into his life story. He was within an ace of finishing mine.

He'd managed to get his switchblade out of somewhere. His idea was to marinate my throat in my own blood. I had hold of his wrist as he had hold of mine. But he knew he had me. He was in a hurry, and started to gargle with glee at the thought.

I had enough reserve left for one final waltz. I let him get the point of his knife within a half inch of my throat, indicating that all my concentrated effort was focused on preventing him from closing the gap. Then I scissored hard with my right leg, his trapped inside, and rolled to the left.

The action brought us slamming against a stack of cartons. Some of them came down on us. They didn't do any damage, only enough to jar him, so that I was able to yank my knife arm free and drive Hugo into his shoulder.

He pulled back with a guttural sound and tried to return the favor, but I'd rolled clear slashing his arm as I went. His blade unzipped one of the cartons. He didn't know it, but at the moment he could have me for tea. I was fresh out of everything. The lack of time saved me. He had none to spare if he was going to continue his career. He came up on his feet, his square, heavy-featured face contorted, wild with rage. "You son of a bitch!" he snarled, and threw his knife.

His aim was good. It was his rotation that was off. I caught the haft of it in the chest. He vaulted the cartons. I scrambled, looking for Wilhelmina, aware of the wild roar of the crowd and the futile wail of an ambulance.

His headstart was a good one, and he was being pursued by a zombie. The material used to seal the tunnel entrance had been a thin layer of plywood. He had gone through it like a clown through a circus hoop, tearing apart the makeshift structure.

I went down into the unlit tunnel. I could hear him scrabbling ahead of me. I held my fire until the floor leveled out. The sound of the shots blasted through the darkness. They brought no outcry, no answering fire. We both knew the layout; knew that we would be forced to a crouch, but once he got around the tunnel's elbow he was almost home free.

I had two shots left when his muffled shout came back to me. He was close to the escape point and was calling on his comrades to give him a hand. I couldn't catch what he said, but I needed no Baedeker to explain.

I was panting hard when I reached the turn. The blackness was inside me as well as out. He was getting away, and I was fading out. You're a great Killmaster, Carter. Why don't you retire!

I came around the angle and heard more voices. Some light filtered down, enough so that I could make out the bulk of the president killer's body. He stood on a ladder.

He wasn't climbing out—he was getting something. I steadied Wilhelmina. I saw him step down and turn, making a motion with his hands together. I fired twice. He buckled and grabbed at the ladder, shouting for help. Then he made a weak underhand pitching motion with his right hand. No one had to explain that it was a grenade. I heard it plop in the dirt. Now he was howling for a helping hand.

I had the angle of the tunnel wall to protect me from the shrapnel. The force of the blast was something else. Groggy though I was, I was a fair piece back down the tube before the thing went off. The sound made trap drums out of my ears and beat my brains to jellied consommé. That part I could handle, but not the effects of the blast on the tunnel. It began coming down behind me, and then all around me.

No spider ever did a better scuttle. But even a spider has to breathe, and every breath I took was full of dirt and debris. Spiders are apt to get stepped on, too, and I was being stepped on and clobbered by supports and shoring. I went down three times before I was able to stand and really get knocked flat. It was not conscious thought that got me to the upward slope, where a clutch of hands fastened on me and dragged me like a dirty sack out of the tomb.

CHAPTER 29

Die Welt's banner headline read, MAYOR KOLTZ SHOT. The *Morganpost* had it: U.S. PRESIDENT ESCAPES ASSASSIN'S BULLET. There were a lot of variations in between, but from where I lay in the CIA safe house, the rest was academic. Until I spoke to Hawk.

"The President called to convey his thanks." His voice, spaghettied through the scrambler, sounded somber. "Have you anything on N12?"

"Lubiyanka. *Détente* being what it is, I should think he could be extracted. We can let the Kremlin know that the press might like the real story unless he's exchanged."

"I have half a mind to let him sit there," he grunted. I didn't add, "For at least twenty-four hours."

"My target got away," I said.

"There'll be another day. How are you?" He tried to make it sound noncommittal and succeeded.

"I'm still digging dirt out of my ears. I'll be departing tomorrow. How are things there?"

"Buttoned up. We'll talk about it. And Nick . . ."

"Yes, sir?"

"Extend my best wishes to Fraulein Raeder."

I did that and left her sitting up in her hospital bed surrounded by flowers and telegrams, looking winsome and a bit choked up that I wasn't going to be staying. Aside from the big news—the Mayor shot in the leg and the President unharmed—she was the big news. Everyone in West Berlin was proudly singing the praises of the student group that had brought off the biggest unpaid-for escape from East Berlin in years. But it was Hilma Raeder whom they had taken to their hearts, and before she could get hold of some part of mine, I kissed her a chaste farewell and got out of there.